Harriet Jane Hanson Robinson

The new Pandora

A drama

Harriet Jane Hanson Robinson

The new Pandora
A drama

ISBN/EAN: 9783337335335

Printed in Europe, USA, Canada, Australia, Japan

Cover: Foto ©Andreas Hilbeck / pixelio.de

More available books at **www.hansebooks.com**

THE NEW PANDORA

A DRAMA

BY

HARRIET H. ROBINSON

NEW YORK & LONDON

G. P. PUTNAM'S SONS

The Knickerbocker Press

1889

Press of
G. P. PUTNAM'S SONS
New York

THE NEW PANDORA

" It fell in the ancient periods,
    Which the brooding soul surveys,
Or ever the wild Time coined itself
    Into calendar months and days."

PERSONS REPRESENTED.

PANDORA—The first woman.

AETES—A primitive man.

CHARLICO
HARMONIA } Children of Pandora and Aetes.

OLEN—A Norseman, lover of Harmonia.

HOPE.

EPIMETHEUS.

VULCAN.

TWO CYCLOPS.

SOPOLIS, POLITES, PELIAS, LYCÙS, MICCUS, DOLOPS, STILPO, BIAS, DION, CLEON, ASBOLUS, SAON, and KURNUS— Primitive men.

SCENE : Greece in the primeval age.

" It fell in the ancient periods,
Which the brooding soul surveys,
Or ever the wild Time coined itself
Into calendar months and days."

PERSONS REPRESENTED.

PANDORA—The first woman.

AETES—A primitive man.

CHARLICO
HARMONIA } Children of Pandora and Aetes.

OLEN—A Norseman, lover of Harmonia.

HOPE.

EPIMETHEUS.

VULCAN.

TWO CYCLOPS.

SOPOLIS, POLITES, PELIAS, LYCUS, MICCUS, DOLOPS, STILPO, BIAS, DION, CLEON, ASBOLUS, SAON, and KURNUS—Primitive men.

SCENE : Greece in the primeval age.

PROLOGUE.

"But Jove our food conceal'd : Prometheus' art
With fraud illusive had incens'd his heart :
Sore ills to man devis'd the heavenly Sire,
And hid the shining element of fire.
Prometheus then, benevolent of soul,
In hollow reed the spark recovering stole :

. . . . . .

'O son of Japhet !' with indignant heart
Spake the cloud-gatherer, 'O, unmatch'd in art !'

. . . . . .

'This fire shall draw perdition on the race,
And all enamour'd shall their bane embrace.'
  The Sire who rules the earth and sways the pole
Had said, and laughter fill'd his secret soul :
He bade the crippled god his hest obey,
And mould with tempering water plastic clay ;
With human nerve and human voice invest
The limbs elastic and the breathing breast;
Fair as the blooming goddesses above,

A virgin's likeness with the looks of love.
He bade Minerva teach the skill that sheds
A thousand colours in the gliding threads:
He call'd the magic of love's golden queen
To breathe around a witchery of mien ;
And eager passion's never-sated flame,
And cares of dress that prey upon the frame ;
Bade Hermes last endue with craft refin'd
Of treacherous manners, and a shameless mind.

.   .   .   .

Then by the feather'd messenger of heaven
The name Pandora to the maid was given ;
For all the gods conferr'd a gifted grace
To crown this mischief of the mortal race.
The Sire commands the wingèd herald bear
The finish'd nymph, th' inextricable snare :
To Epimetheus was the present brought,
Prometheus' warning vanish'd from his thought—
That he disclaim each offering from the skies,
And straight restore, lest ill to man arise.
But he receiv'd; and conscious knew too late
Th' insidious gift, and felt the curse of fate.
    Whilom on earth the sons of men abode
From evil free and labour's galling load ;
Free from diseases that with racking rage

Precipitate the pale decline of age.
Now swift the days of manhood haste away,
And misery's pressure turns the temples gray.
The woman's hands an ample casket bear;—
She lifts the lid,—she scatters ills in air.
Hope sole remain'd within, nor took her flight,
Beneath the casket's verge conceal'd from sight.
Th' unbroken cell with closing lid the maid
Seal'd, and the cloud-assembler's voice obey'd.
Issued the rest in quick dispersion hurl'd,
And woes innumerous roam'd the breathing world."

.   .   .   .

The Works and Days—HESIOD.

ACT I.

THE NEW PANDORA.

ACT I.

SCENE I.—*A cave in the earth, in which are standing a huge anvil and forge, a rude stone bench, and a tripod holding a small brass ewer.*

Enter VULCAN *and the two* CYCLOPS, *bearing a mass of clay, which they lay on the bench.*

VULCAN.

Mould soft, mould fine the dainty clod.   Add myrrh,
Frankincense, nard, the rose's cheek.   A lock
Of starry gold, the violet's purple eye,
The veinèd marble's blue, its creamy white :
'T is something finer far than common clay.

CYCLOPS, *kneading the clay and pouring, now and then, from the ewer.*

We 'll stir, we 'll mix, we 'll mould with care
The tempered clay, with motion rare ;
We 'll knead the mass, with strength refin'd,
This source of ills to all mankind.
Who Jove would circumvent,
Himself he cheats, ha ! ha !

11

Sly Prometheus stole golden fire,
And great Jove laughed in secret ire,
And bade us form, with artful grace,
A mischief for the mortal race.
    Who Jove would circumvent,
    Himself he cheats, ha ! ha !

  [*The clay has gradually assumed human shape ;
  the feet are well defined.*

VULCAN.

Raise up the form and stand it on its feet,
That I may finish what high Jove commands.
Leave me alone; I would with tranquil mind
Fashion this form that is to cheat mankind.

  [*Exeunt* CYCLOPS. VULCAN *stands on the bench
  and moulds the clay until the beautiful head
  and bust of a maiden appear.*

  SCENE II.—*A path leading down a mountain side.
Olympus at the back, " snow-covered and rose-
crowned."*

  Enter EPIMETHEUS *and* PANDORA, *bearing a
  large casket. They set it down.*

EPIMETHEUS.

Dost thou remember who created thee ?

PANDORA, *hesitatingly.*

When first I oped mine eyes, and saw the day,
I stood afar upon the mountain height ;
Nor knew I aught ; and gods and goddesses
Encircled me and bade me lift mine eyes.
I looked, and joyous life informed my veins.
Then stepped a goddess forth, and o'er my form,
Pulsing with life, a snow-white garment laid,
And o'er my head a veil, and round my brow
A coronet, embossed with curious shapes.
Another hung about me golden chains ;
And then the bright-eyed Hours around me threw
Garlands of spring, fair meadow blooms, the hues
Of primrose yellow, daisy white, all blent
With violet's flush and sad Narcissus' smile,
While creeping up and down the flowery wreath
The sun-eyed pimpernel looked shyly forth,——

EPIMETHEUS, *interrupting.*

Yes ; but, my child, didst thou not know thy fate ?

PANDORA.

My fate ? Oh, no ! And what should be my fate ?
I only know that life is sweet. All day
Through happy fields or sunny vales I roamed,
Companion of the white-winged messengers.
Minerva wise, taught me to weave the web
With colors gay, that interlace and glide
Within each other, like the glancing leaves.

Fair Aphrodite gave me many a gift,
And all the gods conferred on me a grace,
And I was named Pandora, all-endowed.

EPIMETHEUS.

Did not fleet Mercury, that led thee forth
From high Olympus, tell thee of thy fate ?

PANDORA.

Oh, no !   He bade me walk with him adown
The vale.   And on the way strange words he said :
That I must go with thee to some far land,
And carry all the gifts the gods had given.
And mine as well, said he.   *And I endow*
       [*She hesitates.*
Thee now with wily falsehood, tricksy ways,
With speech insidious and with shameless mind.
And then he left me and I walked with thee
To this fair spot, and this is all I know.

EPIMETHEUS, *meditating.*

So ! from the lips of this too guileful god,
There comes the first of evil thoughts to thee.
        [*Aside.*
Poor child ! and must I tell thee of thy fate ?
        [*To her.*
No woman ere had lived on earth until
Thou cam'st, and men have lived from evil free.
No toil have they, no baneful care, no pain,

Nor have they known of dainties hid in earth,
Or healing herbs.   Mallow no virtue hath,
Nor yet papàver's sleep-inviting juice ;
For angry Jove hath kept them from their eyes
Since was the time my brother angered him.

PANDORA.

Thy brother angered Jove, the god of gods ?

EPIMETHEUS.

Prometheus was the friend of man.   He strove
In plans 'gainst Jove, and with illusive art
And fraud incensed the god (in sacrifice
He kept the better part for man ; to Jove
He gave the bones, the semblance of the ox).
And Jove, to be revenged on mortal man,
Hid deep the shining element of fire.
But Prometheus, benevolent of soul,
Who sought to help mankind, o'er-reached great
    Jove,
Stole fire from heaven to light the abodes of men.

PANDORA.

Stole fire from heaven !

EPIMETHEUS.

                Yes, child, and thus it happed
My brother brought down this great good to man :
He was a Titan's son ; Clymene gave
Him birth,—a nymph of Ocean's dancing stream ;—

He ever thought that Jove ill-treated man,
So tried to help him, teach him how to live.
This : and for that he stole the fire, he lies
Enchained on craggy rocks of Caucasus,
And evermore the eagle's beak doth rend
And daily feast on his undying heart.

PANDORA.

Is there no help?

EPIMETHEUS.

    No, none. So all must fare
Who Jove defy, or bend not to his' will.

PANDORA.

Ah, me ! How came it that he stole the fire ?

EPIMETHEUS.

One day he stood by sea-green Ida's mount
And Jove defied, saying : *I fear thee not ;*
For man I strive. His good is more to me
Than tranquil bliss with thee and all thy gods.
Then spoke the angry god in thunder tones ;
With fierce bolts sought to stab Prometheus' heart.
But he, with courage grand, undaunted stood ;
Tight in his hand a fennel stalk he bore,
And high in air he held it to the sky,
When through its hollow tube, white-hot with rage,
Jove's bolt was hurled. It stabbed the ground.
  He fell.

Soon he arose, alert.   The yellow flame
Had caught the low-hung bush, the tawny grass
Embraced, and seized the hollow tree.   Aloft
It strove, and crackled all around ; it burned
With jocund flame.   Prometheus seized the prize,
And, shut in chambers dim, laid it to rest.
And now, in men's abodes, or hollow caves,
It lies imprisoned fast, for man's own use.

PANDORA.

But what hath this to do with me ?

EPIMETHEUS.

Hearken,
And I will tell.   When Jove beheld the fire,
He laughed in scorn and said : *O man, exult*
Thou not in triumph over Jove.   This fire
Shall draw perdition down on all thy race ;
An evil shall be wrought, a beauteous snare,
A mischief dire to thee, inventive man !
He called to Vulcan (halting in both feet,
The artist god, maker of forms of things),
Bade him with water temper plastic clay,
And make a beauteous maid, who, seeming fair
And good, to mortal man should yet bring ills,
Bring sorrow, pain, and care to all his kind.
That maid art thou !   For this thou com'st to
     earth !

PANDORA.

What ! *I* bring ills to man ?   What ! *I* the source !
I ne'er knew ills, why should I be their source ?

EPIMETHEUS.

So Jove decrees.   A seeming blessing thou,
But yet a curse——

PANDORA.

       What ! I, a curse ?   Great Jove !
Oh, why did he a woman me create ?
And why, in high revenge for that the son
Of fair Clymene stole the fire from heaven,
Should I, too, bear the blame ?   It was not I !
I did not ask to live.   I had no choice.
Ah, let me go !   Back to Olympus' height,
And leave this clogging, weary earth behind !

EPIMETHEUS.

It may not be.   Olympus' mount is left
Far off, remote.   There was thy place of birth,
(Who touches heaven before he lives, and brings
Its radiant memories with him, sure is blest !)
And ne'er again until dissolves in dust
Thy toil-worn clay, wilt thou its summit reach.
Thy lot is earthly life, with man to live.
Go ! live thy life appointed.   Do not ask
The reason why, nor question Jove's behest.

PANDORA.

Why didst thou take me from bright Mercury,
And lead me here to earth?

EPIMETHEUS.

It was my fate.
In spite of what my brother said,—to take
No gift from Jove, for in it lay a snare,—
I thee received. For that I brought thee here
To earth, adown the track of time my name
Will hateful be. I shall be called " pur-blind "
And " Epimetheus of the erring mind."

SCENE III.—*An open glade. At the back* AETES,
LYCUS, SOPOLIS, MICCUS, *and other men, lying on
the ground. Some are eating ; others wrestling.*

Enter EPIMETHEUS *and* PANDORA.

PANDORA.

What are these forms I see? They look like gods,
Yet rough and wild, with tangled hair and beard.
Low on the ground they lie. Such shapes I ne'er
Have seen while on Olympus' mount I dwelt.

EPIMETHEUS.

These shapes, my child, are men, thy mates.

PANDORA.

My mates!

EPIMETHEUS.

Yes, they are made of clay like thee, not clothed
As are the gods.   But yet, as 't was with thee,
The will of Jove called them to life.   And they
Inhabit this fair earth at his behest.
A few are good, some bad, indifferent some.
Thee hath he sent to live and do as they.

PANDORA.

I live and do as they ?. I, who have been
The blest companion of the white-winged gods ?
Great Jove, have pity !   Let me not be sent
Of thy revenge th' unwilling instrument !

SCENE IV.—*A woody spot with tangled underbrush,
and a rill of water.   At the front a hut roofed with
bark and open on all sides.   Mount Ossa in the distance.*

Enter PANDORA *and* EPIMETHEUS, *bearing the
casket.*

EPIMETHEUS.

Here will we rest.   Undo the casket's rim,
And scatter forth the ills that thou hast brought.

PANDORA.

Why must I lift the lid and scatter ills ?

EPIMETHEUS.

It is thy fate.   Obey, nor ask me why.

[PANDORA *lifts the lid of the casket.   Cloudy*
shapes arise and vanish from the hut.

EPIMETHEUS.

Are all the ills abroad?

PANDORA.

Yes, all abroad
Save one ; one yet remains within the verge.

EPIMETHEUS.

'T is Hope, a seeming ill, but yet a good.
Shut down the lid.

PANDORA.

Why may not Hope come forth?

EPIMETHEUS.

Not yet.   When all thy life with man is done
And thou and he, raised to an equal height,
Subdued, uplifted, disciplined, refined,
Stand side by side beneath the arching blue,
And both can see the meaning of your lives,
Then will sweet Hope come forth (when thou dost
     will)
And dwell with man upon the breathing earth.

And now I leave thee.   Thus far have I brought
A tender maiden toward a woman's lot.

> [*Exit* EPIMETHEUS.

> [PANDORA *leans dejectedly against the hut.*
> *Cloudy shapes are seen flitting to and fro at the*
> *back.*

CHORUS OF ILLS.

Away we float, to brood on the earth ;
  Settle, settle, on land and sea.
In the darkness of Hades we had our birth,
  Breeding, seething, untiringly.   .

DISEASE *speaks.*

I shall live in the fens, in the sea-green mould,
  Lurking, lurking, in pleasures gay ;
The maiden fair and the youth so bold,
  And the new-born child, I shall steal away.

SORROW *speaks.*

I shall blanch the cheek, and whiten the hair,
  Eating, eating, the heart's core out ;
Bend the mother's form, blight the maiden fair,
  Break the father's pride, make all men doubt.

PAIN *speaks.*

I shall twist the limbs and shorten the breath,
  Racking, racking, the whole day long ;
Waste the infant's life, bring to beauty death,
  Make youth seem a cheat, and age a wrong.

CARE *speaks.*

I shall bend the neck with an unseen pack,
  Carking, carking, at every ear ;
I shall wrinkle the forehead and bow the back,
  Make life a burden and death a fear.

TOIL *speaks.*

I shall harden the hands, bind the face to the sod,
  Grinding, grinding, in life's hard mill ;
And man shall be changed to a slave and a clod,
  Toiling forever his mouth to fill.

ALL *together.*

Away we float, to brood on the earth,
  Settle, settle, on land and sea ;
In the darkness of Hades we had our birth,
  Breeding, seething, untiringly.

PANDORA, *who has been listening in terror, steps forward.*

Great Jove ! what had I done ? What rage refined
Made me to bring these ills on all mankind ?

SCENE V.—*The same ; with an ilex tree in the foreground. In the centre of the open hut is a rude bench, on which lie a dead kid, a gourd, some dried fruit, figs, bunches of grapes, etc.*

PANDORA *wearily.*

He bade me food prepare ere he should come.

[Takes off her flowers ; they fall to pieces in her hands.

Poor flowers ! your day was short, your life was
    brief !
How fades the primrose sweet, how dim the eye
Of violet looks ! And columbine, her leaves
Of vermeil hue, droop like my garments' pride.

*[Takes off her veil, coronet, cestus, and ornaments,
  and hangs them at a corner of the hut.*

Fair veil, that decked my virgin brow, by wise
Minerva wrought, your fleeting day is done !
And ye, my jewels rare, and coronet,—
Hang where ye will. For me thy golden pomp
No more will gleam. Gone my companions all !
And far away, Olympus lies, my home,
Where I, in maiden freedom walked, nor cared
To change my lot. Ah me ! no more to sup
At banquets fine, nor drink of nectar full
The crystal cup, at tables set for gods !
O my lost life ! How can I thee forget,
And dwell with man, or ever be his mate !
How I do loathe this place—this common earth
Where I must dwell,—the life I 'm doomed to lead !
Last night, when I was left within the hut,
Aetes came. When me he saw, and viewed
The casket o'er, and heard my story sad,
He murmured and complained to all the gods

For sending such a gift ; for that with me
He must accept the ills.   Oh, I would fly !
But where ?   The vale is full of men.   This morn
I saw them prowling round the hut wherein
I hidden lay.   Oh, I do fear this man
Who me reluctant takes, nor thanks the gods !
Ah, why, great Jove, hast thou created me ?

> [*Takes off her mantle and appears in a white
> tunic.*

When forth Aetes went and left me here,
Before my sight he seized a trembling kid,
And, rending it in twain, he said : *Clean this ;
Prepare the food, and when I come from chase
I 'll eat my fill.*   I ne'er did this before.

> [*She takes a flint knife and tries to flay the kid,
> but gives up in disgust.*

I cannot eat raw flesh.   I ne'er did that.
The gods have taught me I must eat baked food.
Ah me ! I have no fire !   Where is 't ?   What said
Old Epimetheus ?   *Now, in men's abodes,
In chambers dim, or hollow caves, it rests.*
Great Jove ! If I must suffer thus that man
May have his fire, O let me share the good !

> [*She comes out of the hut and kneels beneath
> the ilex tree. A little bird sings and twitters
> over her head. Being all-endowed, she has the
> power to understand its language.*

What saith the bird ?   *Rub two sticks ! rub two sticks !*
Will that bring me bright fire ?   I 'll heed its song.

> [*She rubs two pieces of wood together, and a spark appears.*

Behold, the fire !   Now can I bake the kid
And eat.   'T is yestermorn since I did eat.

> [*She reënters the hut, cuts off a little piece of the kid, and puts it on the fire.   She then draws a log from outside the hut and places it at the bench for a seat, brings a gourd of water from the rill, gathers some leaves, and is arranging the fruit when* AETES *enters, and throws himself on the ground.*

AETES.

What hast to eat ?   Where is the meat, the fruit ?
Bring all to me, that I may eat my fill.

PANDORA.

Wilt thou not sit ?

AETES.

I ne'er did sit, but ate
My food from off the earth.   'T is better so.

PANDORA.

The gods all sit at table when they eat.

AETES, *roughly.*

Well, if thou wilt.　　　[*Sees the meat on the fire.*
What 's that ?

PANDORA.

'T is meat, for me.
I ne'er did eat raw flesh, nor can I now.

AETES.

Thou 'rt mighty fine !　'T is good enough for me.

PANDORA.

Yes, but among the gods I ne'er did eat
Raw flesh.　The gods do not ; 't is not their food.

AETES.

We are not gods : we eat the food of men.
Bring me the grapes ; the water fetch.

[PANDORA *waits on him.　He makes a great ado
eating and drinking, and spills the water.　She
silently offers him a leaf to wipe his beard.　He
flings it down in disgust.*

Woman !
Wilt thou not eat ?　You live no more with gods.

PANDORA.

I cannot eat as thou dost.

AETES.

As thou wilt.
Eat thy baked meat alone, and be content.
It seems I do not suit thee ; and my ways .
They do not please thee.   But thou 'lt ne'er forget
That thou no more dost live with gods, but men.
Remember, thou art sent to live with me.
Make of 't the best thou canst ; and so will I.
And now I leave thee, and I haste with speed ;
Instead of one mouth I have two to feed.

[*Exit.*

PANDORA.

Remember ?   Would I could forget the fate
That brought me here as thy unwilling mate !

ACT II.

ACT II.

ACT II.

SCENE I.—*Same as Act I., Scene V. The under-brush is cleared, and the hut, which is at the back, is closed on all sides. Over the door are trained rose and clematis vines, and near the entrance flowers are planted.* AETES *sits outside the door making a rude plough.* PANDORA *sits beneath the ilex tree holding a child, and singing softly to herself.*

PANDORA'S LULLABY.

Sleep, softly sleep,
　　Little woman-child,
On my aching heart,—
　　Still its tumult wild.
　　　　　　Sleep, softly sleep.

Sleep, gently sleep,
　　O fair be thy lot !
My sorrowful fate
　　O follow it not !
　　　　　　Sleep, gently sleep.

Sleep, sweetly sleep ;
　　The ewe on the lea

31

And the doe hath her young,
And I, only thee.

Sleep, sweetly sleep.

Come, tranquil hour,
Low-laden with sleep,
Come, gentle zephyr,
And watch o'er her keep.

Sleep, baby, sleep.

[*She rises, goes past* AETES *and enters the hut.
He looks after her.*

SCENE II.—*Inside the hut. There is a shelf with
gourds, wooden spoons, flint knives, etc. In the centre
is a low table on which are meat, barley cake, and
fruit. A rude loom stands in one corner, near which
is suspended a baby's hammock, or cradle, made of
skins. The casket is at the back.* PANDORA *stands
near the hammock.* AETES *sits in the doorway at
work on his plough.*

PANDORA, *turning to* AETES.

I dread the coming of these men, so rude
Are they.   I hear them oft within the wood,
And hide myself, and fear the child will cry,
And they will enter, when thou art away.

AETES.

They 're not all rough.   Some are as good as I.
[Or as I was before thou cam'st.]   And would
Be well behaved did they not live alone.

[*Enter* LYCUS, SOPOLIS, POLITES, *and* MICCUS, *former companions of* AETES. *They throw themselves on the floor of the hut.* PANDORA *offers them wreaths.* AETES *puts his on his head.* POLITES *follows his example, while the others examine theirs curiously.* PANDORA *offers food to all.*

SOPOLIS.

What is this myrtle for, so twisted up ?

AETES.

It was the custom in the woman's home
To twine the brows of guests with wreaths.
She doth
It in remembrance of the gods, her mates
Aforetime, for 't was so they sat at feasts.
[*Aside.*
Confound those gods ! That Mercury I hate.
She dwelleth oft upon his ways, repeats
The nonsense soft he poured into her ear.

MICCUS, *putting his wreath on the back of his head.*

I wonder which god 't is I look most like ?

SOPOLIS.

It must be Bacchus, come without his goat !

LYCUS.

See how he eats !   He cuts the flesh with knives,
And in his maw he places little bits,
As if 't were berries small or cornels red.

SOPOLIS.

See how he sits !   The earth, it seems, he scorns !
He doth not eat the flesh he giveth us.
Say, what is that thou 'rt putting in thy maw ?

AETES.

'T is flesh that 's baked with fire,—the woman's way.

MICCUS.

Dost like it ?

AETES.

So—so.   *She* doth think it good.

MICCUS.

Oh !   She doth think it good !   A pretty use
To make of fire !   I 'd rather keep its flame
To warm myself, when chill Boreas blows ;
Bake my own haunches, not the kid's soft flesh !

[PANDORA *hands some dried fruit and berries, on
a large leaf.*

LYCUS.

What is this leaf for, put beneath the figs ?

AETES.

To drop thy champings in,—not on the ground.

MICCUS, *derisively.*

Is this the woman's way ?   Dost thou like this ?

AETES, *aside.*

I think, mayhap, 't is needless, but 't is so
She likes it.

LYCUS.

Then 't is so must we !   (*Aside.*)   Mayhap !

[*They finish eating, and* SOPOLIS *and* MICCUS
*pull some long green leaves out of their tunics,
cram them into their mouths and chew, spitting
around.*

AETES.

Be careful where ye spit !   She doth not like
It done within the hut.

LYCUS.

What stuff !   I 'd teach
Her, very soon, that I would do whate'er
I choose ; have my own way ; that she should do
As *I* should please, and that my word was law.

[*The child makes a little cry.*

What 's that ?

AETES.

It is the child.

LYCUS.

What child hast thou ?

MICCUS.

Where was the man-child found ?

AETES.

'T is not a man,
It is a woman-child.

MICCUS.

Where found you it ?

AETES.

I found it not.   'T is hers—and mine—our child.

MICCUS.

Her child and thine !   Did it not come as we ?
Didst thou not find it hid in hollow woods,
Or mountain dells, or in some flowery bed
Of parsley or of thyme ?

AETES.

No, 't is her child.
The woman gave it birth, e'en as the doe

Brings forth the dappled fawn, the goat her kid,
The ewe her yeanling, and the kine their young.

[*The men all look with wonder on the child.*

LYCUS, *laughing.*

I ne'er did hear of aught so strange ! But 't is
The woman's way, no doubt, with all the rest.
'T is deep enough ! She leads him like a sheep !

[*Seeing* PANDORA'S *veil, mantle, and ornaments,
he puts them on and says, mincingly, to* AETES.

Is this the way she looked when first she came ?
And did she smile, like this, and sweetly say :
*Aetes, I have come to live with thee,
To lift thee from the ground, to make thee sit
And eat thy food, and bake it, if I please.
And thou must chew it ;*—as if thou wert sick
And loathed it, not with relish strong, and smacks
Of chops, that show how toothsome 't is and good !

POLITES.

See how the woman shakes ! Thou shouldst not
   fright
Her thus ; keep thou thy antics for thy mates.

[AETES *smiles a little, but* PANDORA *retreats toward the child's cradle.*

LYCUS.   ·

What is 't to thee ?   I 'll see how she doth shake !

[*He goes up to* PANDORA, *and attempts to take
hold of her arm.* AETES *flies at him, knocks
him down, and drives him from the hut. The
others follow,* POLITES *with an apologetic ges-
ture.* AETES *fastens the door and turns toward* PANDORA, *who is standing, in terror, by the
cradle.*

AETES.

Thou 'rt safe !   But mind, if one of them should
    come
When I 'm away, bethink thee which one 't is.
I 'll teach him that if *woman's ways are deep*,
There 's something in a man that 's more than
    sheep.

SCENE III.—*The same.* PANDORA *sitting listlessly
near the loom. In her hand is a little child's shoe
made of white fur. Enter* AETES, *who goes to the
cradle, looks into it, touches the child, and starts back.
He then looks all round the hut, as if searching for
something.*

AETES.

Where is the child ?

PANDORA.

Ah me !   I do not know.

[AETES *looks again into the cradle, partly lifts the child, groans heavily, and then turns fiercely toward* PANDORA, *who shrinks from him.*

AETES.

What ails the child ?   What hast thou done to it ?

PANDORA.

Indeed, I know not.   I have nothing done.

[*She falls at his feet, weeping and moaning.*

This morn, when thou didst quit the hut and left
Me sorrowing here, at all the words, the taunts,
We both did use, the child set up a cry.
I heeded not, but made my plaint to Jove,
And mourned for lost Olympus, where I strayed
In virgin freedom, nor had wished to roam—
A careless maiden, with unthinking mind.

AETES.

The child ! the child !   Thou woman, where 's the
    child ?

PANDORA, *unheeding.*

But fate, stern fate, and Jove's command, brought
    me
To this low hut, this common life.

AETES.

The child !
The child ! What hast thou done with that ? Where
   is 't ?

PANDORA, *still unheeding.*

And I did curse great Jove, with bitter cries
For that he made me woman.   And the child
Cried out again.   Unto my breast its lips
I laid ; it drank and in my face it smiled.
'The agony was gone from out my heart,
But ah ! the child felt all the pang.   Its head
Back in my arms it laid, its face grew dark,
Its breath went out, its snowy limbs grew still.

AETES, *angrily.*

Thou woman, source of all my ills !   For thee
I toil all through the weary day.   Once, when
I wanted food, I seized the flying fawn,
Tore out its heart, drank of its blood.   Well-fed
Was I.   But now I flocks and herds must tend,
Must till the earth, and snare the tender bird,
That thou mayst eat and thrive.   I happy lived ;
And if I dirty was, as oft thou sayst,
I was enough content.   I knew nor toil
Nor care ; nor knowledge had,—but lived in peace.
Now thou dost make me bear long days of toil,
And suffer sorrows, ills, and pains untold.

PANDORA, *rising.*

I cannot help that Jove created me ;
Would he had not, or left me in my home
Where erst I dwelt in bliss.   There broke the morn
With songs, the hills responding echoed back
The strain ; fresh came the food prepared for gods ;
Like clouds the garments grew.   But now my days,
So full of pain, I pass in thy rude hut,
With frets and cares new-born, ,and grief un-
    plumbed !
In toil and sorrow must I ever live.

AETES, *looking again into the cradle.*

Thou woman ! Jove did make thee for a curse.
For this he sent thee, and he has his will.

PANDORA.

I did not wish to come to thee, nor stay
When I was brought ; nor did I want the child.
It was thy will that gave it us, not mine.

AETES.

What is 't thou sayst ?   Wert thou not sent to me,
As was the ewe, the mare, the mottled doe ?

PANDORA.

Oh yes, I am the same !   The mare, the ewe,
The mottled doe, no choice of owners hath.
No more had I !   But they have seasons, times ;

They bear their young with willing joy.   But I
Alone, thy mate and not the brute's, have here
No choice.

AETES.

But I will have thee for mine own.

PANDORA.

Thou dost possess the clay, made far below
In Vulcan's workshop, but it is not I !
That, Heav'n-born, still eludes thee, tho' thou
    tread'st
Its mould to dust.

AETES, *in surprise.*

I did not know thou hadst
A thought like this——

PANDORA.

Thou didst not ask, nor care
To know how hard it is for me who dwelt
Aforetime with the gods, to drudge for thee,
To care for all thy needs.

AETES.

——And that thou wast
Not willing to become my mate.   Is 't thus ?

PANDORA.

I was not asked !

AETES.

And art thou not content?
Thou hast enough to eat, art housed and fed?

PANDORA.

Thou 'rt born of earth, and canst not understand!
Dost thou not know that still around me clings
My heavenly birth?   That thou art not as I?
Oh, I would rather be the mate of him
Who whispered in my guileless ear the first
Alluring words!   Or Epimetheus!   He,
Though old and blind, were better far.   They both
Are god-descended, or of Titans bold.
But thou!   No glimpse of god-like birth I find
In thee!   From far-off heights no sun-light comes
To enter thine abode.   How can I be
Content?

AETES.

Then will I leave thee, here to dwell
Alone.   And I 'll go live with my old mates
Thou call'st *the wild men of the woods.*

                              Go thou
To Hades—and for aught I care.   Or else
Go back to thy high-dwelling home again;
Go back and find your lying Mercury!

                              [*Exit* AETES.

PANDORA.

Ah me!   I cannot go, nor ever more
My earthly feet will tread its heavenly floor.

SCENE IV.—*The same.* PANDORA *alone.   She goes to the child's cradle and looks in.*

PANDORA.

Where is the child ?   Indeed, where is the child ?
Its form is there, just as mine was before
I oped mine eyes on those remembered heights ;
Just as I was when Vulcan carried me
From out his workshop dim.   But where the voice,
The smile, the joy, the loving looks, the life ?
Where are the pulses warm that filled its frame,
The ways so sweet that lightened my sad life ?
I know not.   Neither do I know from whence
It came.   What is this thing, not made of clay—
The life !—that laughs and sings, despairs and
      weeps ?   .
Where does it go ?   To what far land I ne'er
Can reach, has gone what erst I called the child ?
Oh ! ice-bound feet no spring can loose, where is
The power unseen that led thee forth alone ?

[*She sits down wearily at the loom.   Invisible
      spirits sing over the body of the little child.*

SPIRITS.

Come away !   First-born child of an earthly maid,
   Come away to the valley of rest.
Come and play where the flowers like stars are laid.

LITTLE CHILD-SPIRIT.

I would sleep on her soft-falling breast.

SPIRITS.

> Come away !
> Unwelcome hast thou been, and cold on thy brow
> Rest the eyes that should look only love ;
> Sweet bud, thou wilt bloom where the still waters
>   flow
> In the green shining pastures above.
> Come away !
> Come away ! In his mercy Jove calls thee away.

LITTLE CHILD-SPIRIT.

> Oh, no, no, I would stay ! I would rest !

SPIRITS.

> We wait for thee : thou must no longer delay.

LITTLE CHILD-SPIRIT.

> Let me sleep on her soft-falling breast.

SPIRITS.

> Come away !

PANDORA.

> My child, my child ! Thou art indeed my child !
> I falsely said, when in my grief and pain,
> That thou wert not my child ! Go not away !
> Or take me with thee to the unseen land.

SPIRITS.

Come away, child, 't is for thee, not thy mother,
  We leave her to sorrow and pain.
When the hard day of life for her is all over
  We 'll unite you, forever, again.

Come away !

LITTLE CHILD-SPIRIT, *feebly.*

Let me stay ! Let me rest
On her soft-falling breast !

[*The song dies away and* PANDORA *sinks to the
  ground.*

SCENE V.—*A glade, in which are several huts,
some better than others. Rude farming implements
are scattered around, and some goats and cows are
tethered in the background.* LYCUS, SOPOLIS, MIC-
CUS, POLITES, PELIAS, STILPO, *and* KURNUS *are
seen, some busy with their farming implements.* POL-
ITES *is mending a net, and* MICCUS *is playing with
the animals. Enter* AETES.

LYCUS.

Why, here 's Aetes !   He 's come back again !
How haps that thou dost deign to visit us ?
Or, hast thou come to live with men, and be
A man's companion, not a woman's mate ?

AETES, *hesitatingly.*

Mayhap !—I 've come to stay awhile, that is——

SOPOLIS.

Bring forth the meat, the ripest figs, the grapes ;
'T was so we fared when we did visit him.

[*Brings out meat, fruit, etc.*

LYCUS, *aside.*

I well remember how *I* fared that day.
But I 'll repay !   If he the woman 's left,
Then shall she be *my* mate.   (*Aloud*)   Give him the
   best.
With open arms the welcome guest receive.

[*The men sit on the ground,* AETES *on a little
   mound.   They eat in a rollicking way—all but*
   POLITES *and* PELIAS—*throwing the bones and
   grape-skins at each other.   AETES does not eat
   the meat ; but sits in a dejected attitude, eats a
   few grapes and mechanically drops the skins
   into his right hand.*

SOPOLIS, *observing* AETES.

Seest thou, his dress no longer is like ours ?
But tricked with colors gay, like autumn leaves
Of oak or chestnut when they drop their balls ;
Or yellow hamamelis' dancing plume.

LYCUS.

She made it.   'T is the woman's work ; her will
That tricks him out, just as she doth bedeck
Herself.   She fair and comely looks, by Jove !

MICCUS.

If we lived in Aetes' hut, we should
Be forced to eat baked meat, our champings hold
Within a leaf, not throw them on the ground,
Or at each other, in disport and play ;
Nor could we chew the long green plant in peace.

LYCUS. .

Not on the ground, said he. *She likes it not !*
Ha, ha ! I wonder if she 'd like it now.

> [*To* AETES, *who does not notice what the men say,
> but sighs and is silent.*

Why dost not eat the meat we eat ? Thou 'lt find
No baked flesh here. No woman's ways with us !

POLITES, *aside*.

Would that we might, to quell such swine as thou !

AETES.

I know it well. Thou need'st not bruit it forth.

> [*He groans aloud.*

MICCUS, *aside*.

I ne'er before heard man make such a noise !
'T is like the cow that cannot find her calf ;
'T is like the mare that mourns her foal when lost.

SOPOLIS.

He ne'er did seem like us. Last spring, thou know'st,
Just after we all met the assembled gods
(And Jove had led her forth—but she saw not—
And wonder seized the immortal gods—and us—
To view this snare 'gainst which men's arts are
    vain),
He left our haunts and built a hut apart.
As if Jove's messenger had said to him :
Thou 'lt have a woman mate and thou must make
A place for her abode. He seemed to expect
A gift not known to us, from highest Jove.

MICCUS.

And so it was he made a place for her ;
Just as we did for fire Prometheus brought.

LYCUS, *laughing.*

And he is scorched by her, as we are scorched
When oft we play with fire. And that is why
He 's fled. She 's baked him, as she did the kid,
With her soft tongue, her speech, her *woman's way !*
And let this saying be, for all mankind :
He who with fire plays, or woman dwells,
Will dread the flame and ever feel the smart.

POLITES.

I think not so, for oftentimes I wish
That Jove had sent us more, aye, one apiece.

And then like strong Aetes could we live.
We should not herd like beeves, but dwell like gods,
Apart, alone, each with his own true mate.
And round our fires might gather little ones,
The playthings, the companions of our sports.
But now the fawn, the foal, the kid, the calf,
Are all we see of youth or blithesomeness.

[LYCUS laughs aloud.

PELIAS to LYCUS.

It ill beseemeth thee to say such words
Of her !   Who sent thee cloth to bind thy wounds ?
That *she* did weave ; the healing balsam made.
What knew we of the virtues hid in herbs,
In thyme, in asphodel, or lily root,
In sage or bay, to cure our ills and hurts ?
Prometheus said these things were good, but we
Ne'er tried them till she taught us to distil.

STILPO, a blind old man.

She doth no good to me.   I 'm full of pains.

LYCUS.

Nor would she, though 't were Dian's horn she
     brought
Filled full of healing herbs.   Thou 'rt past all cure.

MICCUS.

Methinks no change hath she e'er made in me.

LYCUS.

Methinks thou couldst not be improved, although
The gods themselves sent down perfecting herbs.

POLITES.

A man is blest who hath a woman mate,
Who liveth aye with her, who hath a child.

MICCUS, *laughing.*

Polites oft is searching for a child. '

POLITES.

Thou need'st not laugh.   I freely own that I
Do want a child ; have sought in wood and field
To find a mate.   I live but half a life.
Without a mate and child, a man is like
A crippled tripod standing on one leg,
The pestle that no mortar hath, the flail
That lacks the handle, or the sharpened axe
Without the helve, the bellows and no forge,
The lanthorne dull that hath no flame within.
He 's like one half the fire-tongs, or the shears
That undivided clip the fleecy wool.

LYCUS.

A good conceit !   She 'd clip *thee* fast enough.

POLITES.

Think what the change would be, if to our world,
The world of men, should beauty come and grace !

We live like russet trees, bereft of leaves
When winter reigns—a dingy life, and worse—
As men must always live when they do dwell
Alone.   Were women pure, and children here,
Our world would bloom, as if from every bush
And barren bough, rhodora red should burst
And fill our scentless lives with sweet perfume.
                                                [*Aside.*
I know not why the god sent me no mate.
Nor what did strong Aetes do, that he, not I,
Should be so blest.   [*Reverently*]   It was the will
     of Jove.

AETES, *to himself.*

I did not know that she was not content,
That she unwilling was to be my mate.
I thought, if she were housed and clothed and fed,
It was enough,—that like the abandoned fawn
Of dam bereft, she would caress the hand
That fed, and follow willing where it led.
I did forget her heavenly birth, ignore
Th' imprisoned thing that, couching in her clay,
Resisted and defied me.   O great Jove !

SOPOLIS.

What doth he say ?   What makes him thus ?   I ne'er
Have seen him, since he drove us from his hut.
What aileth him ?   And why hath he come here ?

LYCUS.

He 's with the woman lived, that 's all, I think.
I 've seen him oft. I hoped the other day
To see the woman's face again, and learn
If women children had increased within
Aetes' hut ; so stole among the trees
And through the branches peeped ; and at his door
I saw him stand. He held the woman-child,
And thus he dandled, tossed it up and down,
And sang :

Uppy, uppy, baby goes !
Downy, downy, baby goes !
Little piggies are his toes,
See his little nose !

The baby laughed and I ran off.

[*All laugh boisterously.*

AETES, *rousing himself.*

What is 't thou sayst ? And didst thou speak to me ?

LYCUS.

Yes, we did ask thee where the woman is ;
If thou hast left her still within the hut ?

AETES.

And if I have, then what is it to thee ?

[*Relapses into his dejected attitude.*

LYCUS.

If he has left her, then shall she be mine.

SOPOLIS.

No, mine !   I 'll fight for her !

MICCUS, *meekly.*

I have no chance.

[LYCUS *and* SOPOLIS *struggle together and go out.*

POLITES.

I 'll follow, hinder them from harming her.

[*Exit.*

PELIAS.

What ails thee, man ?   Arouse thy strength ; take
　　cheer.
Thou wert the bravest, strongest one of all.

AETES.

Leave me, good friend ; I cannot talk with thee.
Thou canst not say the words to cure my hurt.

[*Exit* PELIAS.   MICCUS *seats himself on a
　　mound, imitating the attitude of* AETES, *and
　　makes several attempts to groan.* AETES *starts
　　up and* MICCUS *runs off.*

AETES, *looking after him.*

Was I like that ?   Companion of the goat
And kine ?   Did I so live—before she came ?
What if she did bring ills ?   How mean in me
To tell her so !   She brought me comfort too ;
She made my burden light, she brought the child.
It was not hers, nor did she want the child,
She said.   Ah me !   And yet I wonder not
She did not want the child of one like me—
So rough and coarse, who seized her as his prey
Nor thanked the gods, nor asked her own consent !
And yet, I did not know—how could I know—
A man should sue, not seize, his woman mate ?
I must go back ;   I cannot live with men,
Since I have shared the life that woman leads.
We must together dwell.   My life is naught
Apart from her.   Jove sent her for a curse ;
But I would rather have her as she is,
Than all the nymphs, yea ! all the goddesses.
Thou Highest God ! beneath thy intended ban
A blessing manifold was hid for man.

[Exit.

SCENE VI.—*Outside the hut, which is securely
closed.*   LYCUS *is prowling about and goes up to the
door.   Enter* AETES *with his head down.   He looks
up, sees* LYCUS *and springs upon him.   They struggle
desperately,* AETES *conquers, and drags* LYCUS *off.*

SCENE VII.—*Inside the hut.* PANDORA *alone.*
*The door is securely fastened and the loom is drawn
up against it. A noise and scuffle are heard outside..*
PANDORA *tries to hide behind the casket. After a
time all is still and she comes from her hiding-place.*

PANDORA.

How long a time it is, since I was left !
I have no food.   I am afraid to go
From out the door.   Now he is gone, I fear
Those wild men of the woods. He drove them off.
I did not think that I should miss him so,
Or care for his return.   How can I live ?
> [*A noise is heard at the door, and then a timid
> knock.* PANDORA *starts.*

AETES, *softly.*

Pandora, wilt thou not undo the door ?

PANDORA, *relieved.*

'T is only my—Aetes !   Hast come back ?

> [*She tugs at the loom and unfastens the door,
> but retreats to the farther end of the hut.
> Enter* AETES *with some wood, a water-gourd,
> some dressed meat, and bunches of grapes.*

AETES, *putting down the supplies.*

Yes ! I 've come back to live with thee—if thou
Dost please—since thou still dwellest here. I sought

The glade where men resort ; but all their life
Seemed rough and gross, remembering mine with
 thee.
I could not bear their habits wild, their talk
Uncouth, their ways. The thought of thy sweet face,
Thy winsome voice, and thy warm presence near,
Caused me to fly. I 'm rude and coarse, I know,
But I will try to grow more fine ; take on
Thy gentler manners and thy softer ways,
Thy habits rare—

PANDORA, *interrupting.*

What sound was that I heard
Outside ? I have so feared,—since thou wert gone.

AETES.

It was that Lycus who did visit us,
Who donned thy mantle fair, and called me *sheep !*
I knocked him down, thou know'st, when he did
 touch
Thine arm.

PANDORA.

At early morn, I heard his voice
In loud command : *Come, woman, forth !* he said.
I answered not, but silent lay within
The hut.

AETES.

I caught him prowling round thy door.
I 've sent him where he 'll never prowl again,

To seek *thee* out, or touch thy tender arm !
I could not live with such as he, since I
Thy presence knew ; and then,—the child, the
    child !—

>   [*Approaching her.*

One thought of e'en the spot where first it drew
Its breath, where its soft voice was heard—it is
More dear to me, than all the world outside.
Here, where it lived and died, let me too live
. And die.   Oh, I 've been watching round the hut
All through the weary night, so that no harm
Might come to thee and it—the child, *our* child !

>   [*He comes nearer to* PANDORA, *who shrinks
>   from his approach.*

Oh, fear me not !   I will protect thee, get
Thy food and care for thee ; but nevermore,
Until thou say'st, will I again e'en touch
Thy violet finger tips.   Thou art not mine.
'T is not for me to seize my Heaven-born mate,
But wait her coming to these welcoming arms.

>   [*He holds out his hands, pleadingly.*

I will forget the ills—they seem as naught ;
Without thee, love, I can no longer live.

PANDORA.

Do not forget the ills I brought.   They are
For me, as well as thee ; to both they come.

But when thou wouldst reproach me, ne'er forget
I 'm not to blame, and that I had no choice.

AETES.

I will not !

PANDORA.

    Then I 'll strive to be content.
Forget my words. Since on the earth we must
Together live, I will no longer mourn
For my lost home, nor pine for a return ;
But live, and meet our common lot with thee.
Let us no more each other taunt, but try
To bear together all the ills I brought.

AETES.

Yes ! We 'll begin our life anew. And in
Our home shall dwell nor strife nor discontent.

PANDORA.

And I will trust thee—as I have not done,—
Confide to thee my sorrows and my fears.
Wilt thou not help me do as I would do ?

AETES.

I will, thou mother of my child ! And we
Will make our home th' abode of happiness ;
And both together we will teach great Jove,
That these, his ills, can be made goods to us.
But, dear Pandora, wilt thou not love me ?

PANDORA.

It may be—if I can—when thou lov'st me !

AETES.

I do love thee.

PANDORA, *looking down.*

                    Not as I would be loved.
Who loves, forgets himself, oppresseth not
The one he loves ; doth more than clothe and feed,
And find a home for his own mate. He doth
Consult her wishes, honor her, respect
Her feelings, as they were his own.   True love
Sustains the mind and makes the spirit thrive ;
Uplifts the earthy toward the spiritual part.
It makes the dullest clod a thing of life ;
Its presence fills the darkest hut with light,
Illumes its walls of clay.   It silvers o'er
The wooden spoon and gilds the gourd with gold.

AETES.

And if I love like this, wilt thou love me ?

PANDORA.

If thou art kind, I 'll learn to love thee well.

AETES, *joyfully.*

Then hasten, love, to find our poor abode !
Come dwell with us, eat of our common food !

PANDORA, *looking up at him.*

And love will conquer pain, make sorrow joy,
Disease and toil an easy load, and smooth
The brow of care.   Such love I 'll give to thee,
When thou lov'st me.

AETES.

Great Jove, thou 'rt foiled again,
With thine own weapon, made of fragile clay!

PANDORA, *stepping toward* AETES.

And then, when all the ills shall in our hands
Change into blessings rare, mayhap will Hope—
As old and purblind Epimetheus said—
Come forth and dwell with man upon the earth.
Hope, that will show the way where our first-born
Hath gone ; Hope, that will teach us, though we still
Must toil and sorrow here, we oft may rise
Above our cares and reach serenest heights.

AETES, *taking* PANDORA'S *hand.*

Dear mate, weep thou no more !   I know a spot
In Tempe's vale, quiet and deep.   There will
We take the child and cover it with flowers
That thou dost love.

PANDORA.

Yes, we will give the child
To mother earth, to rest within her arms,

Its clay to clay.   There, all day long the birds
Will sing, and bees from far Hymettus come,
And rosy clouds from my lost home will make
A fleecy covering for its little bed.
But, Oh, it is not there ! For in my heart
Doth something truly say, that far away
In some unclouded land we cannot see,
The feet we miss, now bound and still, unchained
Will be, and free.   And when our earthworn steps
Have reached their journey's end, they 'll follow
      where
To higher paths the little child doth lead.

                              [*Exeunt, hand in hand.*

ACT III.

ACT III.

ACT III.

An interval of twenty years is supposed to have
elapsed.

SCENE I.—*A hut covered with vines and roses. The
grass is green in front, and the path to the door is bor-
dered with flowers.* PANDORA *and* HARMONIA *are
spreading a web of cloth on the grass.* CHARLICO
*sits at a little distance carving a piece of wood. A
bunch of flowers is beside him, at which he looks from
time to time.*

PANDORA.

Spread out the web, my child, and let the sun
With warmest beam make white each slender thread.

HARMONIA.

Why, mother dear ! The rain is in the sky,
And o'er the tree-tops high, on Ossa's mount,
Dark clouds and misty shadows drooping lie.

PANDORA.

Thou needst not fear. The sun will come, for all
The signs are out. 'Way down the northern sky

A strip of blue, just large enough to make
A mantle soft for thee, doth lie.   The smoke
From out the fire that cooked the morning meal
In curling wreaths ascends.   The emmet red
Hath cleared her doorway of obstructing sand,
And rounded out the arching roof that hides
Her galleried home.   The spider small, on bush
And o'er the bending grass, his kerchief, gemmed
With morning dew, hath spread.

HARMONIA.

           How canst thou tell
The signs? I know them not. Though all the signs
Of earth should speak, I should not know their
    voice,—
And still should ask of thee.

PANDORA.

           Last night, didst thou
Not see, low in the west, the line of blue?
And mark the amber clouds, like burnished gold,
That hung far up the sky?   The morning gray
The evening red succeed?

HARMONIA.

           Are these the signs?
Then, mother dear, what are the signs of rain?

PANDORA.

At early morn, when thou dost see the sun

Come clear and bright from out his bed, and then,
Within an hour, behind the clouds to hide :
A morn when sharp and clear, and on the grass
The frost doth lie in silver flakes : A noon,
When deeply blue without one cloud, the sky
Is seen ; or when, as is the thunny's back,
Flecked clouds appear : A night, when in the North
Shoot up the flickering lights like lances bright,
Or all the sister Pleiads shine undimmed ;
When evening gray precedes the morning red,
Or Amalthea's shed an odor gives,—
Within a day a watery sky will fall.

HARMONIA.

My mother dear, how many signs there are !

PANDORA.

Yes, all are good ; but yet do all signs fail,
Of weather wet as well as dry, in heat
As cold.   But we must still have faith ; and trust
To Mother Nature's voice.   Her lessons speak
In earth and sky, in every bud and flower,
If we do hear aright, attune our ear
To her soft speech, interpret her true word.
                [*They spread the web.   Exit* HARMONIA.

PANDORA, *to* CHARLICO.

My son, thy father doth not need his plough
So gayly carved.

CHARLICO.

Fair forms unbidden come !
Straight lines I cannot make ; they all are curved.

PANDORA.

Go forth into the vale, drive home the goats,
And bring the evening wood.

CHARLICO.

It is no use.
I 'm good for naught but dawdling here with thee.
Where 're I go, my fancies still pursue.
When at my work, in wood or field, I dream ;
When others sleep, I wander far away
To shadowy realms informed with visions rare
I ne'er have seen on earth. The morning's red,
The evening's light, is full of radiant shapes ;
In every flower a face I see. They come,
They follow me, are my companions still.

PANDORA.

My son, my Charlico, my mother-boy,
Inheritor of my etherial self !
Hear thou my words. For that thou art a man,
Must live with men and learn their ways, I speak.
Sometime, somewhere, mayhap, thou 'lt find a mate.
Then make a home for her and thee ; and this
Will cause thee to forget thy wandering dreams
In happy confidence of mated life.

CHARLICO.

The Dryads and the Oreads have no charms,
Nor yet the Nereids, daughters of the sea.
I see them oft—the blithe Glauconome,
And Halimede, with her beauteous wreath,
Evarne, rosy-armed Hipponoé,
And Ashnymphs, guiltless born, of Earth and
  Heaven.
They lure me not.   There is no mate for me.

PANDORA, *aside.*

Thus did I dream in those first lonely years.
Thus longed I, ere I knew Aetes' heart.

CHARLICO.

But I have seen a face.   'T is fair like thine,
Its hue, of sunset pale, its radiant hair
Is twisted gold and curls like Jasmine's vine.
But ah ! it flies, eludes me, when I wake.

PANDORA.

My Charlico, 't is but a wandering dream.

CHARLICO.

All things in Nature go in pairs.   Each bird,
Each animal hath its own counterpart.
The flowers ne'er bloom alone.   The blades of grass,
The odorous trefoil, in procession walk
With their own kind along the upland field.

In saddest hours I oft in silence lie
Among these countless shapes.   They rear their
      blades
In thousand pinnacles, that lean and nod
Each unto each, a thronging company
That ever reach to embrace, and trembling lie
Within each other's grasp.

PANDORA, *aside.*

                    What art of mine
·Can break th' illusive spell that o'er him broods,
And warps his life ?

CHARLICO.

                    The clouds go hand in hand,
Receding down the sky, past Dian's bow ;
Together sink they in the slumberous West.
And e'en their shadows 'cross the planted field
Swim side by side.   All have their mate but me.
I walk alone ; 't is this that makes me grieve.

PANDORA.

O my poor son !   Why wilt thou not go forth
Where men resort, and learn their ways (if good),
Learn courage, self-reliance, gain new strength,
And teach thyself to be a man with men ?

CHARLICO.

Aetes' son is but a dreamer born.

                                    [*Exit.*

PANDORA, *after a pause, wearily.*

I am not old, yet all my body wanes.
My hands, that once were plump, have shrunk like
    ears
Of Autumn corn. It wearies me to cook
The daily meal ; the care of herbs and flowers
It is a task. My plodding heart doth thud
With heavy beats against my side ; my feet
Are slow as are the snails that on the sands
Of ocean leave their spiral track, in shape
Like visible speech of man or bird. No help,
No virtue, hath the terebinthine juice
Of liquid amber, nor a cure in herbs.
The healing Althaia's cup contains no balm.
Not all the simples grown on Pindus' side
Can reach my hurt, for grief doth age a form
More fast than do the years. O first-born child,
Untimely sent from earth ! thou art my hurt
Incurable, the source of my decay.
Ah me ! in vain I try to think it out.
Not her earth-life alone, but lives mayhap
Of thousand others, that from her might spring,
A long procession of fair, sinless babes
Adown the countless years. O innocent child !
How could thy mother e'er forget that thou
Wast not to blame for coming into life ?

Enter AETES, *with gourds of fruit.*

AETES.

Here is the last of all our fruit, that plucked
And stowed away through all the winter's cold
In our deep cave, hath stood the season's chill.
See how the orange looks, all shrivelled, wan,
And wimpled like an old man's cheek !

PANDORA.

                                    The quince
And pear, how wrinkled they, and tough ! Their
    hide
Is like the crawling skin of Tauros old.

AETES.

And see ! The fig, pomegranate, and the grape,
They look like—well !

PANDORA.

    Much past their bloom—as we !

AETES.

But, never mind. We 've had our time of bloom,
Of mellow fruiting, and of season ripe.
Now we renew our youth and live again
Within the forms of our two children dear.

PANDORA.

Yes, I do live indeed within my son.
My nature he doth have, and all my ways.

He is not bold, as I would have him be,
Nor strong, like thee ; but he is full of dreams,
As I have ever been.   And even now,
I ofttimes lose myself in visions bright,
Forget the passing hour and all its dues.

AETES.

Thou ne'er forget'st my coming home ; my days
Are brimmed with thoughts of how thou 'lt look,
      when I,
With weary feet, come up the homeward path.

PANDORA.

When at my loom, all thro' the warp and woof
Of my poor web, I interlace my dreams ;
See marvellous scenes within its fabric gay,
And splendid pageants all unknown to earth.
This narrow hut expands, and I do seem
Not in its bounds, but in a peopled world.

AETES.

Sweet love, among thy fancies wrought, O let
My face, thy loving mate, sometimes appear !

PANDORA.

It doth full oft.   Thy goodness and thy truth,
Thy love, I weave, and then the beam shines clear,
Illumined by thy worth.   I see thy brow
Serene, thine eyes so pure, so brave.   Within

The mesh doth hover oft thy smile ; and then
I wake, and try to serve thee well.

AETES.

Too well

Thou servest, and too much thy life is given
To me and mine, that I may comfort know,
That we may all in woven robes be dressed.

PANDORA.

. Thy life is real ; thou dost till the earth,
And up the mountain side the deer dost track,
And snare the fleet-winged bird ; with net or spear
Dost seek, by ocean's wave, the gliding bleak.
Where men assemble, thére thy voice is heard,
And more and more they list to thee, to judge
And settle their complaints.

AETES, *laughing*.

And ofttimes, too,

When some do my decisions doubt, they say :
It is the woman's voice that speaks thro' him
For peace alway !   No fights when she is round !

PANDORA *continues*.

But I, instead of filling all my hours
With useful toil, am ofttimes lost to earth
In day-dreams vain,—and so my Charlico.
The beautiful is more to him and me
Than well-filled garners, or than flocks and herds.

AETES.

I 'm glad he is like thee. I ever wished,
Tho' I a hundred children had, they might
Be all like thee, and not like me. Enough
There are as I. But Spirits rare, that spring
Of heavenly birth, descend from off the heights
To inhabit this low earth, are few indeed.
If thou hadst worldly-minded been, as well
As heavenly, thou wouldst know too much to live
With me, thou wouldst not be my willing mate.
Thou 'rt mated with a pigmy small, a hind.
Thou art like Pegasus, brought down to earth
And yoked and harnessed with a common steer,
Or Phœbus' car, switched off the heavenly track
Beneath the common shed where wains are kept.

PANDORA.

My wondrous mate, how high thy fancy flies !

AETES.

I am the pack-horse, thou the bird that soars
And sings, and wends its way, ere Winter comes,
To other lands, and finds eternal Spring.

PANDORA, *aside.*

He doth not think it may be thus with me ;
He knoweth not my way is marked for flight.

AETES.

Yet all are needed to make up the world.
If all were fine, then who would till the soil,
And plant and gather food to feed mankind?
If all were coarse, then beauty were unknown;
No joy and comfort, no blest lives, no homes
On earth be found, nor children born of Heaven.
I love thee as thou art. For all the world
I would not have thee changed; and day and night
I thank the God that thou wert made for me;
And ofttimes smile and hug myself, and say:
FOR ME, did Jove send her with ill intent
To earth; *for me* did Vulcan mould her clay;
For me, within his darksome cave did blend
Rhodora's red, Viola's blue, to grace
Her eye and cheek. She lives! to earth she came
For me, for me! I am the happy man!

PANDORA.

My dear Aetes!

AETES.

          Let the boy dream on!
We have enough for all. He doth not need
To lead a life so full of toil as mine.

            [*Taking* PANDORA *by the hand.*

Let us go forth.   I saw this morn some flowers
Like those that thou didst wear within thy wreath
When first thou cam'st to make complete my world.
I left them there (thou know'st my careful ways,—
I never wanton pluck their blooms, to tread,
As some men do, their broken lives to dust,—
I love to see them nodding on their stems).
But thou wilt like to gather them to adorn,
To beautify our home,—as oft thou dost—
And then I see thee as thou wast that day
When first thou cam'st to earth, a beauteous maid,
To me wert given, to evermore be mine,
And make my lowly hut resplendent shine.

[They go out.

SCENE II.—*Woods surrounding an open glade.
Ossa at the back.   Enter* HARMONIA, *panting, and
leading a white doe with a rope of grass.*

HARMONIA.

A merry chase thou 'st led me, Iole !
From steep to steep, I followed thee adown
The wood embossed side of Ossa's mount,
And jocund Zephyr tracked our flying feet,
And reaching Dryads caught my flowing hair.
My pretty doe, wilt thou not speak to me,
And tell me when the fair-haired comes this way ?

HARMONIA'S SONG.

Iole ! Iole !
My Iole, now tell me true,
 When will the fair-haired come this way ?
With manly shape and eyes of blue,
 With stature tall, and step so gay ?
    Iole ! Iole !

In thy soft ear, my pretty doe,
 I 'll tell thee all my secret plan ;
'T is this—and I will speak it low,—
 Mayhap I 'll love this fair-haired man.
    Iole ! Iole !

Away, away, my Iole !
 Go whisper softly in his ear,
Tell him what I have told to thee ;
 A mortal maiden waits him here.
    Iole ! Iole !

     [*The doe makes a little noise.*

What saith the doe ? My mother dear its speech
Would understand. I cannot. I 'm earth-born,
Not all-endowed as she. But yet, enough

    [*Enter* OLEN *unseen, at the back.*

For earthly life—'t is so my father saith.
Yet would I know what speaks swift Archelous,
As on he flies past Pindus' peaceful glades ;

He sweeps the crinkled shadows of the woods
Adown his path, and louder far he sings
Than all the rhythmic runes the wood-nymphs
   hymn.

                [*She unties the doe.*

Away she bounds ! Would I were born of Heaven !
Would I were like my mother dear ! Then I
Should know the language of the woods, the waves,
The speech of bird and arrowy-footed doe.
But my inheritance is all of earth,
'T is swiftness, vigor, ruddy health and strength.

    [OLEN *springs forward and attempts to seize her.*

Away, rude man ! How dar'st thou seize me thus.

OLEN.

I want thee ! Woman aye was given to man !

HARMONIA.

It may be so ; but not unless she wills.

OLEN.

Thy father seized thy mother—so 't is said.
I thought it was the way.

HARMONIA.

               'T is not the way,
At least with me ! My mother had no choice ;

Jove willed it so.   But he no longer wills
That maids be seized by men, unless they choose.

OLEN.

I 'll buy thee, then !   I 'll to thy father give
My sandals shod with gold, my spear, my bow
Of strength.

HARMONIA.

          Thou canst not buy my father's child !
My father's spirit dwelleth deep in me,
'T is my inheritance.   I 'll not be seized,
But will my freedom keep.   Now go thy ways,
And learn to speak a maiden fair, and when
Thou thinkest best to *sue*, I 'll answer thee.

OLEN.

Be not so angry, I have loved thee long.

HARMONIA.

If thou dost love me, make thyself a man,
Just like my father, or Polites kind

OLEN.

What is 't I do thou dost so much dislike ?

HARMONIA.

Dost thou not chew the dirty weed ?   And then—
Thou followest the nymphs of wood and stream.

OLEN.

[*Takes something out of his mouth and throws it
behind him.*
I do no harm.   And I will grow more mild—
[*Aside.*
I 'll never speak with one of them again,—
[*To her.*
Learn better habits.   Wilt thou be my wife ?
I 've loved thee long.

HARMONIA.

Where hast thou seen me ?

OLEN.

Here
Within the wood I 've watched thee.

HARMONIA.

I 've seen thee,
A-creeping, prowling round amid the trees.
Thy meaching face did look as looks the sheep,
Or hairy satyr leering from the bush.
[*Aside.*
I did not think so, but he knows it not.
[*To him.*
I never thought thou lookst on me as prey !
Thou hadst a look as if thou wanted food—
Some grapes, or figs, or kids ; but not a mate.

OLEN.

But wilt thou not forgive me, list to me?

HARMONIA.

Where dost thou come from, with thy long fair hair?

[*Aside.*

I like it well.

OLEN.

From Northern woods I come,
From Woden's land ; Asgard is his abode.
Within his palace, seated on his throne,
He overlooks the heavens and the earth.
Hugin and Munin on his shoulders sit,
And every day to all the world they fly,
To bring him news of what they 've seen and heard.

HARMONIA.

Oh, I have seen them on the tulip-tree,
And fed them oft with bits of wheaten cake.

OLEN.

I fed these ravens black from earliest youth ;
And, like a curious boy, I listened well
To all their wondrous tales, and in my heart
I pondered them.

HARMONIA.

What name was given to thee,
Thou shepherd of the birds?

OLEN.

I 'm Olen called.
One day they came full freighted to the North.
The news is great, they said. *In sunny lands,*
Where thro' Thessalian plains Peneus winds,
Near high Olympus to the Thermean gulf,
Where Southern gods have their abode, is born
A daughter to Pandora (all endowed)—
The only woman-child of all the Greeks.

HARMONIA.

But I an elder brother have. His name
Is Charlico ; he 's fair, like thee. And then ?

OLEN.

And then I fed the birds full well, and oft
I coaxed them each to tell his tale again.
And in my heart I said : *She shall be mine !*
This mortal maid shall be my own true wife.

HARMONIA.

And why, since thou wast there, didst thou not
    seize
A maid from thine own land ?

OLEN.

I like them not.
They 're not like thee. They are immortals all—
The maids of Woden's land, Asgard's abode,—

They are the Valkyriors, the messengers
Who bring slain heroes to Valhalla's hall.
And when they fly on their strong horses, armed
With shield and spear, their yellow hair illumes
The northern sky—and this foretells that rain
And cold are near.

HARMONIA.

    My mother sees them oft.
It is her sign.

OLEN.

    I ever wished a maid
Of mortals born. I want a wife to stay
At home, and not go flying all abroad.

HARMONIA.

How didst thou know the way to look for me?

OLEN.

Each year, on their return, the ravens brought
Me news of thee. They said : *She walks, she grows
Apace ; her hair is dark, and midnight broods
Within her eyes.* Last year, when they came back
To Woden's land, I fed them well with choice
And juicy bits of Schrimer's side,—the boar
Whose ever growing flesh the heroes eat
Who bravely die, and after feast—and then
Did coax them soft to tell me news of thee.

HARMONIA, *aside.*

How happy am I, listening to his tale !

OLEN.

She is a maiden grown ; she 's tall, they said,
And like the Delian palm, she rears her head.
Her form is lithe, and like Munychia's bow
Whene'er she twangs the string, she doth rebound,
If bent against her will. [*Laughing.*] I 've found
    it so !

HARMONIA.

The ravens know ! With beechen twigs I scared
Them oft, when they my red-winged pigeon vexed,
Or stole the seed-corn scattered near his cote,

OLEN, *resuming.*

Around her limbs, they said, *her chiton falls*
In colors numerous as are in the bow
That Bifrost builds to arch the flood and tell
That rain is o'er. No longer did I wait,
But took the barley cake, dried flesh and fish,
And cheese from milk of red Audhumbla made,
My bow of strength, my double-headed spear,
And came to find thy land.

HARMONIA.

      Did'st safely come ?

OLEN.

I lost my way, and brambles tore my limbs.
Ofttimes wild beasts pursued me, and the heat
Of southern suns oppressed me sore.   But yet
My heart, it ever sang : *Far in the South*
A mortal maiden dwells, and waits for me.

HARMONIA.

How couldst thou know that I would wait for thee,
Nor mate with one belonging to my race?

OLEN.

I knew that thou wouldst ever wait for me.
True love, such love as mine, must find response,—
E'en though the endless years, the earth itself,
Should roll between.   And so for thee I came,
The only wife for me in all the world.

HARMONIA, *aside.*

O joy ! I can no longer hide my love.

[To him.

I did not know that thou wouldst come.   And yet
I thought—*young Dolops—he is not my choice.*
And all my life I will unmated go,
Unless there comes a better man than he,
Who knoweth how to treat a maid.   I hate
His boorish ways, his habits rude despise.

OLEN.

I knew thou wouldst.   But yet, I am, mayhap,
As rude as he in some things that I do.
But I am strange to thee ; and thou, perchance,
Not seeing me, as thou dost him, mayst think
I better am.   I 'm well content thou shouldst.

HARMONIA.

Thou must be better far than Dolops is,
If thou wouldst have me speak with thee again !

OLEN.

Almost a year I 've wandered 'mong the haunts
Of men, have learned their ways.   Far different
      they
From those of heroes brave who come to dwell
In Woden's halls : and some I must unlearn
I fear, if I would gain thy love.

HARMONIA.

Indeed.

Thou must !

OLEN.

But wilt thou love me then ?

HARMONIA.

I will.

No longer can I hide from thee my love.
Because I love thee, and for that alone,

Will I become thy wife.　And yet not then,
Unless my father and my mother will.
Come thou with me, relate to them thy tale ;
Ask their consent.

OLEN.

Thy father fear I not.
I 've met him oft in councils of the men.
It is thy mother that I fear to ask,—
She is so all-endowed !

HARMONIA.

Thou need'st not fear.
The all-endowed doth aye with favor look
On those who are less gifted than themselves ;
And treat with kindness those not blessed as they.

OLEN.

Then will to me thy mother kindness show.
And thou wilt favor, love me, be my wife !
Although thy mother *all-endowed* may be,
Thou 'lt ever be the more endowed to me.

[*They go out together.*

SCENE III.—*Inside the hut. Another room, with rustic seats and tables, some carved in an artistic manner. The cradle is in one corner, covered with a white mantle. Saffron curtains edged with red divide the room from that beyond.* PANDORA *enters and sits down wearily. Enter* DOLOPS (*a young man*), *and* MICCUS, *who goes about looking at every thing in the room.*

DOLOPS, *peering around.*

Is strong Aetes here ? I see him not.

[*To* PANDORA.

Good morn to thee ! How fares the woman-child ?

PANDORA, *startled.*

The woman-child ? What dost thou mean ? My
heart !

DOLOPS.

Thine own Harmonia. She 's well-grown and fit——

PANDORA, *aside.*

I thought he meant the child aye lost to me.

[*To him.*

And what wouldst thou with her ?

DOLOPS.

She 's fit to mate
With man. I ask for her. (I would not *ask*,
But that I fear the strong Aetes' arm.)

PANDORA.

My bright Harmonia mate with such as thou !
No, never ! And 't is well her father hears
Thee not. He 'd say thee nay in more than words.

MICCUS, *who has been slily examining the cradle.*

I see none here.   There is no woman-child.
I wonder where they keep them now.   Dolops
Has come for one.   How wroth he 'll be when he
Finds out that none are here saved up for him.
    [Chuckles to himself and continues the search.

DOLOPS.

Thou need'st not be so wroth ! Harmonia doth
Consort already with such mates as I,—
With one at least.   She 's often in the woods.
With Olen of the North I 've seen her walk.
He held her hand, embraced her form and kissed
Her mouth and blooming cheek.   *[Aside.*
                    I should not dare
To lie like this, were old Aetes here.

PANDORA.

'T is false !   Away ! or I myself will strike
Thee dumb !   *[Exit* DOLOPS.

MICCUS.

            It was not I.   Thou can'st not say
That I did ask for her.   I did not want
The child.

PANDORA.

    No, 't was not thee.   But didst thou see
My bright Harmonia walking in the woods
With Olen of the North ?

MICCUS.

        It was no harm.
Young Olen is a brave and handsome man.
And if he took her hand, embraced her form,
And kissed her mouth, where was the harm in that ?
(I did not see it, but I need not tell.)

       [PANDORA *groans and sighs.*

And now *she* makes the noise Aetes made.
She taught it him ! A fool she makes of him.
I 'm glad no woman e'er was made for me.
       [*Exit. Enter* AETES.

AETES.

What ails my sweetest love, my own true mate ?

PANDORA, *weeping*.

Young Dolops came, and for Harmonia asked
To be his mate. I told him nay ; I said
She should not live with one so rough as he.
This angered him, and sharply he replied :
Already she consorts with such as I.
She is the mate of Olen of the North.

AETES.

Consorts with men ? And walks, unknown to us,
With Olen of the North ? It cannot be.
Or, if 't is true, there 's in it nothing wrong.
A child of thine can ne'er do aught amiss.

PANDORA.

I ever strove to teach her right——

AETES.

Yet still,
She is like me, with instincts strong and wild,
Robust, and full of bounding health.   Within
Her veins doth course a sensuous life unknown
To thine.   She is a child of Nature, free
As air.   But trained by thy sweet hand, the force
That oft, aforetime, did in me o'ertop
My better self, is made to guide and rule
The currents of her life.

PANDORA.

Aetes kind !
I'm glad she is like thee.   I ever wished
My children might be brave and strong like thee.

AETES.

I 'm strong enough—and so is wickedness,—
And yet, I ofttimes think, a character,
In order to be strong, must have a dash
Of darkness in 't, of gracelessness.   This force,
It is a fearful thing.   It is like fire,
A useful servant 't is, if kept within
The bounds ; but if it 'scapes and spreads abroad,
It seizes, devastates all that doth come
In reach.   I 'm thankful that I have no more.

PANDORA.

She may be wilful—but deceitful !—nay !
Nor weak, incapable ! O, much I lean
Upon her stronger nature, as I do
On thine !

AETES.

Yes, I am made to lean upon,
And so, mayhap, is she.   She looks like me ;
She 's dark, and hath my birthmark on her cheek,
The ugly mole thou oft hast teased me with.
'T is a deformity in me ; with her
It is a beauty-spot, it foils the rose
Upon her cheek.   So strong is she, we need
Not fear a fall.

PANDORA.

I know she 's good and true ;
And yet, my heart doth ache to think on what
Young Dolops said.

AETES.

How orderly her ways !
Whate'er she useth, she doth aye put back
In its own place.   Her threads within the web
Are tangled not, but set with even care
As is the order of the standing corn,
Or rhythmic barley bowing in the breeze.
An order-loving nature doth not bring
Disaster to the home ; it doth cement

Its walls.   She honors us, and doth respect
Herself, and e'en for love will not go wrong.

PANDORA.

She ever said : *If e'er I mate, a man*
I'll have just like my father.

AETES.

Yes, and thou
.Did'st answer : *Thou canst not a better have.*

PANDORA.

But these wild men.   They are not like to thee.

AETES.

The breed 's the same.   But in them all I see
A difference.   Some are good, some wild, and some
More tame, and willing to be taught.   'T is hard
To show these men how best to apply the arts
Prometheus taught.   Some take what I impart
As if 't were mother's milk (if that they 'd known),
Like Pelias just, Polites ever apt.
But most ! the thunderbolt of Jove himself
Could not to their dull ears the knowledge break ;
Some learning fear, as 't were a raging boar.

PANDORA.

That foolish Miccus thou didst try to teach
To plant a hedge like thine, tree following tree,
As goats when led by sire or dam adown

The mountain path, each after each ! His trees
Were scattered left and right, and looked like goats
By sudden panic seized !

AETES.

And when I said :
Thin out, make straight thy hedge, 't was done !
   And now
The trees all stand, some here, some there, with
   space
Enough between to drive a fatted ox,
A herd of kine, or millet-loaded wain.

PANDORA.

I could not let Harmonia consort
With men so rude as these. The life they lead,
After her life with us, she could not share.

AETES.

Our home will not be always hers. She will
Not be content. But we must hope the best.
Polites learns the arts with easy grace,
And Dolops, were he not so rough, is deft,
And Pelias, ever just, is loved by all.
This Olen may have traits as good as theirs.
I 've seen him oft. He aye defers to me.
The North breeds noble men ; there Goudan reigns,
And Ask and Emba, man and woman, dwell.
May it not be, young Olen is their child ?

PANDORA.

Thou bring'st the light of morning to my soul !

AETES.

I will go forth, see if she walks with him.
Take heart, remember what I say to thee :
A child of thine can never go astray.
She 's not so good as thou, but good enough
For any man.   I hope for her he 's meet.
Not many men are fit to have a mate,
And very few are fit to live with one.
Thus saith the father !   Thankful may he be
His own dear mate doth not with him agree.

[*Exit.*

PANDORA.

What comfort my Aetes gives to me !
His love doth aye surround me, and he lifts
All burdens from my heart   All, all but one !

[*Reënter* AETES *leading* OLEN *and* HARMONIA.
They go to PANDORA.

AETES.

Thou mother, here is Olen of the North.

OLEN.

Thou all-endowed, thy daughter bids me come
To ask of thee that she may be my wife.
If thou dost will, her father gives consent.

PANDORA

Dost love Harmonia ?

OLEN.

Yes, indeed I do !

PANDORA.

What wouldst thou do for her ?

OLEN.

O, everything !
Take such good care of her !   Will till the earth,
Will hunt and fish, and gather fruit ; will build
A hut, make spoons and knives, [*looking around*]
    a bench, a loom,
                [*Sees the cradle.*
A little cradle, too, mayhap I could.

HARMONIA.

Thou silly goose——

OLEN, *examining it.*
    In truth, I think I could
A cradle make.

PANDORA.
Harmonia, my child——

HARMONIA.

My mother dear——

PANDORA.

—And dost thou love this man ?
Dost thou desire to live with him ? to leave
Thy home, leave Charlico, thy father's arms,
His sheltering care, thy childhood's walks and ways,
The sacred spot whereon thy life began ?
Wilt leave all this and with a stranger go ?
And dost thou love him, child, enough for this ?

HARMONIA.

Yes, mother dear, I do ; and ever shall
While life endures.   I willing go with him,
If thou dost say, unto the farthest verge
Of all the world.

PANDORA.

Thanks be to all the gods !
Then go.   Go thou with him and share his lot ;
Be his true mate.   Go to his empty hut ;
Go make a home for him like to thine own,
To meet the needs of thee and thine.

OLEN.

I think
She will not miss her home.   I 'll love her well.

PANDORA.

Where love abides, that hut is full.   Its roof
With plenty drops ; the poorest vessels made

By loving hands are bright as dishes set
For highest gods. I 'm glad for thee, but grieve
At parting from thee, daughter of my love.

OLEN.

[*Takes* HARMONIA *by the hand and leads her to*
PANDORA.

I thank thee, *all-endowed.* I honor thee,
Thou mother of my love, e'en as I do
The one who gave me birth, and in the North
Waits my return.

[*To* HARMONIA.
Thou first and only one !
Thou first sweet maid of woman born !

PANDORA, *aside.*

That lives !

OLEN.

And thou shalt go with me to mine own land,
To Woden's land, far in the North, to live
Near Ymirs' well that springs from Jotunheim.
Within its depths do wit and wisdom dwell,
And they will teach thee lore of Asgard's halls ;
The song of Bragi, god of poesie ;
How Frey doth make the rain and sunshine fall,
And all the fruits of earth. His sister, too,
Fair Freya, child of music, spring, and flowers,
Breather of love-lorn songs, friend of the elves—

HARMONIA.

I care not for the gods. I 've seen them all.
They only know one thing apiece, can learn
No more : one 's swift, one drinks the wine, one
    plays
The lyre, one hammers, and another fights.
I 'd rather have a *man* can do them all !

OLEN, *taking her hand.*

And my Harmonia shall be ever young.
For there Iduna holds the box which keeps
The apples red, one taste of which doth make
The old grow young, revives a hero dead
To ride his steed again on Asgard's plains.
And over all, in love, Alfadur reigns.
                              [*Exeunt, hand in hand.*

AETES.

Thou see'st, Harmonia could not go astray.

PANDORA.

My wise Aetes ! Thou art right alway.

ACT IV.

ACT IV.

ACT IV.

SCENE I.—*Inside the hut. Enter* CHARLICO *with a pipe of reeds. He seats himself near the casket and plays a melancholy strain.*

CHARLICO.

Why am I not like other men? They seek
The field, the trailing-footed oxen drive,
And till the soil, while I sit idling here.
They rest content, and with dull mind their eyes
See naught in nature but the source of food.
I cannot be like them, for I do know
The secrets of the woods, the abodes where dwell
The daughters nine of Cronos' greatest son.
The dryads and the nymphs of grot and stream
Oft talk to me; the bird, and insect small
That on the bending grass doth plume his wings,
The beasts, the fowls with pinions set that sail
Anear Nomion's car, are known to me.
Yet am I not content, nor satisfied.

[*He repeats the melancholy strain; it is softly echoed from the casket.*

103

What 's that?   'T is like th' Etesian wind that
    breathes
Along the Ægean Sea.

HOPE, *from the casket.*

'T is I ! 't is Hope !

Song of Hope.

I lurk in the gloaming,
    I hide in the night,
I am pining and longing
    To come to the light.

I wait in the darkness,
    O, would I were free !
But to Hope's secret heart
    Only Love holds the key.

As I rest in my prison,
    So fain would I bide
In the soul of my loved one ;
    In his breast would I hide.

Then haste to my chamber,
    Sweet Love ! set me free !
Break the bonds so enchaining
    That keep me from thee.

CHARLICO.

How long hast thou been here ?   I know thy voice,
In dreams I 've heard it, 'mong the woods and vales.

HOPE.

Since first thy mother and the purblind one,
With toilsome steps brought me adown to earth.

CHARLICO.

Why hast thou not come forth?

HOPE.

I am not called.
When I was left within the casket's rim—
The only good, and that a latent one—
Thy mother plead that I might then come forth.
Old Epimetheus said to her these words :
Not yet.   When all thy life with man is done,
And thou and he, raised to an equal height,
Subdued, uplifted, disciplined, refined,
Stand side by side beneath the arching blue,
And both can see the meaning of your lives,
Then will sweet Hope come forth (*when thou dost will*),
And dwell with man upon the breathing earth.

CHARLICO.

My mother oft hath told me this sad tale.

HOPE.

I could not grow while in thy parents' home
Dissension ruled.   But when they dwelt in love,
And with rejoicing hearts brought thee to life—
The longed-for, welcome child,—then I began

To grow.   Then oft thy mother prayed to Jove
That he would bid me forth to dwell on earth.

CHARLICO.

Would I had known it, *I* had bid thee forth !

HOPE.

The time is near at hand.   In all my veins
There throbs a newer life, and in my form
Expands a force that lifts me, till I'seem
To fill the casket full.   But I must stay
Until thy mother wills.   How breaks the morn ?

CHARLICO.

How breaks the morn ?

HOPE.

How opes the eye of day ?
How comes the light to earth ?

CHARLICO.

It softly comes ;
From crevasses unnumbered gently burst
A thousand branching flames, and then the sky
Is all abloom.   Anon, the earth awakes ;
Each form of life that erst was hushed in sleep
Doth sing the morning song.

HOPE.

Tell me the tale,
For I have never heard the morning song.

CHARLICO.

At early morn high on a rock I sat.
Deep grayness covered all, no sound was heard ;
Each little life was hushed in rest.   Silence
So vast, that makes the soul forevermore
Acquainted with its God, slept over all.
And if my spiritual ear could then have heard,
Interpreted the voice that in me speaks,
Then should I once for all have known myself.
But like inscrutable Nature, it was dumb.

HOPE.

How woke the world ?   How found it voice to
     speak ?

CHARLICO.

At first a far-off bird attuned his pipe ;
Then thousands joined the song, and thronged in
     air
A myriad insects swift ; and creatures small,
That always sleep o' nights, came forth to eat ;
The cattle woke and lowed among the hills ;
The zephyrs 'gan their dance.   The rosy Hours
Led forth bright Clarian's car.   He took the steeds
And up the slanting East brought th' advancing
     day.

HOPE.

How looks the world outside? Has springtime
    come?

CHARLICO.

'T is early Spring. The humble shepherd's purse
With footstep round, dots all the plain ; along
The path Arbutus creeps and Vérna lifts
Her head ; in deepest woods the wind-flower hides.
And in the sandy roads, though bruised by foot
Of man and beast, doth Arenària ope
Her dreamy eye. Meadows are carpeted
With daffodil. The air is honey sweet.

HOPE.

How fair, how lovely, is this unseen world !

CHARLICO.

Then wilt thou not come forth and share my life ?
I 've seen thee oft, in clouds, and in the brook.
When Artemis lifts up her gracious head
And through the trees her eye-beams dart,—a path
Of light, I see thy form pass up and down
The luminous way. In thought I follow thee
And oft on rock and tree I carve thy face.
I cannot live unless thou dost come forth.

HOPE.

How didst thou live before my voice was heard ?
How can Love feed on what it hath not seen ?

CHARLICO.

Love needs not see the one it loves. 'T is like
Thyself, impalpable. It feeds on air,
A fancied glance, a sigh, an imagined touch.
'T is of immortal birth, like thee. 'T will live
Long after thine own sweetest self is dust.
This do I offer thee—undying Love ;
The only fitting mate on earth for Hope.

HOPE.

How didst *thou* grow ?   How opes the life of man ?

CHARLICO.

When first I found the *I* in me, and knew
I was not like the things I saw, I stood
And looked far off from out the hut's low door,
Then at the woods, the mountain top, the vale,
The russet kid that rollicked at my feet ,
Then at my hands, my golden hair that fell
Below my knee, my tunic short, my limbs,
My bare and rosy feet, and said :   *These are*
Not I ; for I am this small thing that smiles
And sees, can run, and chase the butterflies.

HOPE.

It was not thus with me. To life I sprang
Complete and full, though dormant long I 've
    lain.

CHARLICO.

And when the *I* in me began to grow,
At first it *wondered*, then it sought to *grasp*,
Then *understand ;* then *fear* and *pride* it knew.
Joy came ; *desire* it felt when first it heard
Thy voice, for then it learned to *love*, and will
Forever after yearn for thee, sweet Hope !

HOPE.

How didst thou know to make the melodious strain,
The first sweet sound that caught my awakening
    ear ?

CHARLICO.

Once, lying on the mount, and listening rapt
To every voice of bird and bee and flower,
There fluttered o'er my head a tremulous breath,
As of a wandering god who passed unseen.
I seized my pipe of reeds, and trembling drew
Such sounds entrancing, as had ne'er been heard
Below the skies.   And then did I *create*——

HOPE.

The notes divine that roused my soul to life
And bade mine eyes behold the light of day !

CHARLICO.

And since that time, I only care to sit
Alone, and breathe the honeyed notes that float
Through secret inmost chambers of my soul.
Would they could lure thee forth to dwell with me !

HOPE.

I come to all mankind, as well as thee,
To make complete thy mother's work on earth.
She is of Heaven.   I am earth-bound.   My path
Is as the bird's, that threads the woods.   Hers leads
To skies remote and near, that span, o'erreach
And hollow in the rounded world.

CHARLICO. '

      If thou
Art sent to help mankind, with me begin,
The youngest, weakest, saddest of them all.
I need thee most.   Come forth and dwell with me !

HOPE.

I cannot, till thy mother wills.   Nor must
I speak to thee again, until the time
Hath come to lead me forth.   This thou shalt do,
For Jove hath willed that Love shall set me free.

CHARLICO.

How can Love live, once having known sweet
 Hope ?
How can Love breathe without its breath of life ?

HOPE.

Tell not thy mother thou didst speak with me,
Or that my coming is so near at hand.
For, though she doth desire me much, she fears

To ask of Jove the promised boon.   In dreams
A messenger to her will come.   I 'll warn
Thee softly of my near approach.   Farewell.

CHARLICO.

O, not farewell !   Invisible thou art,
But go not, go not from my happy heart.

Enter PANDORA, *with a young lamb in her arms.*

PANDORA.

A little lamb, that straying from the fold
Hath lost its way !   I found it in the wood.
Thy father hath gone seeking for its dam.
Canst thou not help ?   What, crooning still alone,
With thy Pandean pipe !   Go, seek the glades
And breathe the air.   Shake off thy listless dreams !

CHARLICO.

I fain would useful be, but 't is in vain.

PANDORA.

My son, go help thy father find the ewe.
Accept thy lot, be more like other men.
Be not so silent, so distraught ; but more
Content to use the gifts the gods do give.

CHARLICO.

Dear mother, I 'll obey ; but ah ! my heart
Will not be there ; nor shall I see the dam,

Nor know her if I do. I cannot tell
A mother-bleat from any common bleat
In all the flock ; they 're all alike to me.

PANDORA.

My poor son ! go thy ways. There is no need.
Thy father doth not want thy help. The ewe
He 'll find a dozen times ere thou dost start.

CHARLICO.

I can no different be, my mother dear.
If thou couldst read my mind, then wouldst thou
    know.

                                           [*Exit.*

PANDORA, *looking after him.*

Useful thou art—enough. 'T is not for me
To blame thee that thou art Pandora's child.
Full well I know that beauty hath its use,
Its place, its lesson in the world ; that 't is
The servant and the friend of man, as much
As labor is.

    [*She makes a bed for the lamb and puts it down.*

                        How beautiful is thought !
It wraps the soul, and makes the body seem
A thing of air ! It knows nor time, nor space,
But free it roams, more swift, more subtile, yea,
Etherial more than are the gods ! Ah me !
I sometimes wish that I had naught to do

But think my thoughts ; and yet amid my toil,
However hard and mean, such fancies rise
As might have had their birth 'midst woods and
    flowers.
And when I make the fire in early morn,
Or sweep the hearthstone up, such glorious scenes
Along the climbing blaze arise, ascend,
As well may fill the sun-god's home, or stream
Through Heaven's blue, adown his shining beam.

SCENE II.—*A bare knoll, surrounded by a circle or
enclosure of stones like a rude forum ; a few mastick
shrubs and chamomile flowers are growing.* AETES,
SOPOLIS, POLITES, MICCUS, DOLOPS *and others.*
AETES *sits on the knoll, the rest are in groups, some
sitting, some standing, and talking in an excited manner.*

AETES.

Now, since the time hath come, if there is aught
That I can settle, give advice about,
I 'll do my best to hear and judge it well.

CLEON.

Sopolis made a fire against my field
And burned my lentils up. Shall fire brought down
For each man's good, be left to burn his food ?

AETES.

Fire should be kept within the bounds.   No man
Hath right to reckless use a thing that 's made

For all.   He should consult his neighbor's needs,
And be as careful of his neighbor's goods
As of his own.   This is true brotherhood.

KURNUS.

I had within my cave wild pears, dried figs,
And cakes well baked, stored up for Winter's use,
When Dion slily came and helped himself.
Shall one man take another's food, as 't were
His own ?   Shall I, with frugal care, lay up
My store for use of cunning thieves ?

AETES.

                              What 's thine
Is thine ; and no more right hath he to take
Thy store, than thou hast right to his.   If we
Allow that stealing 's right, then will no man
Have aught belonging to himself.   'T is thus :—
You steal from me ; I steal from you ; and he
Doth steal from both ; and others steal from him.
Then who owns any thing ?   Possessions aye
Should sacred be ; and what the difference is
'Twixt mine and thine,—the first law 't is to learn.
It doth uphold, sustain the rights of man.

DIDYME.

Kurnus hath set an altar on the plain
To sacrifice to Jove.   What right hath he
To worship there, instead of on the mount ?

AETES.

It matters not where man doth worship Jove,
On mount or plain, if reverently he sets
His altar up.   Not unto sacrifice
Must we set bounds.   Let each man suit himself.

SAON.

My goats did stray, and one, a small one, fought
With Stilpo's old he-goat, and mine was killed.
Shall animals be kept that do this harm ?
That kill defenceless goats when they do stray ?

AETES.

There is a rule all men should know ; 't is this :
When goats oft fight, and bullocks clasp their horns,
It doth behoove their owners that they keep
These creatures far apart and much beyond
Each others' reach.

MICCUS.

                  My ewe roamed in the vale,
And she was set upon by Perses' dog,
And dropped her lamb ; it died.   Shall dogs be kept
To worry neighbors' sheep and kill their lambs ?

AETES.

If thou would'st save thy lambs, make close thy
      bounds,
Secure thy fold and keep thy ewe at home.

DION.

My two milch cows I swapped with Cleon here,
For two fleet mares ; together they 'll not go.
One pulls and jerks, the other stays behind
And balks and plants her feet as firmly set
As is mount Pelion on his moveless rocks.
Shall men exchange good useful kine for brutes
Ill matched as these ?   All men that for me delve
Aye bend the neck, and shall a horse demur ?

AETES.

A bargain is a bargain.   Easy 't is
To govern kine and herds, and men mayhap,
But master of a horse thou canst not be
Unless thou canst control thyself.   A horse
Not mated, should be trained to suit.   The fast
Held in, the slow one urged—he surer is—
The danger lies with him that 's swift ; he needs
The tighter rein ; he 's hardest to control.

DOLOPS.

This Olen of the North !   Shall he come here,
And take the only mortal maid there is
And carry her away ?   She sure should mate
With one of us, of her own race,—with *me*.
I need some one to weave, and make the cake
Of barley wet with honey and with milk.
And she might keep the hut and feed the kine
And hoe the lentils, keep the vetches down.

Too hard I work all through the summer heat,
And olive gathering,—there 's too much for one !

AETES.

If thou hadst wanted her, first in the field
Shouldst thou have been, to gain her own consent.

SOPOLIS.

Well hast thou judged for other men ! Now try
Thy wisdom on thyself ! I fain would bound
My land. It lies in Tempe's vale and near
Peneus' watery bank. I viewed it o'er
And found Aetes here, [*turns to the rest*] our *judge*,
      who knows
What 's each man's right, had planted olive trees
And made a hedge that shaded all my vines
That grow anear the mount. Why shall he plant
On all the sunny spots ? Shall he engross
All Heaven ?

AETES.

                  I thought the right was mine, nor did
I mean to encroach. I 've always planted there.
My mate, Pandora, deems she hath a right
To all the land that borders on the heights ;
That 't is her dower ; 't is her inheritance.

SOPOLIS, *with contempt.*

Thy mate !

MICCUS.

A woman doth not know enough
To have a voice in this—in men's affairs !

DOLOPS.

I 'd like to see *my* mate—if one I had—
Claim her own land !   I 'd turn her from the hut.

POLITES. ⟨

Would that Pandora might be here with us.
Could her soft voice be heard, we should have
    peace.
Her word would settle many points that now
Remain unsolved, for that we do not get
Her side,—the woman view, her thought, her speech.

DION.

Were she *my* mate she should give up her right,—
To land that she doth call her *dower*,—to me.
It seems a woman should obey a man ;
It is the first,—and last thing she should learn.

AETES.

A woman should no more obey a man
Than should a man a woman.   One 's a slave
Who doth obey against the will.   Know this :
                    [*to Dion.*
My mate 's no more my slave than I am hers.
                [*He gets down from his seat.*

SOPOLIS.

If we let her come here, she 'll rule us all.

MICCUS.

I thought her business was to children bear.
'T is long since any came.   She 'd better keep
To that.   I wonder why they don't increase
Within her hut.   *The woman's way*, mayhap !

DOLOPS.

More women children would not come amiss
Now that the Northman 's grabbed the only one.
(But that he beat me in the race, and threw
Me wrestling, I would take her from him yet !)

POLITES, *to* SOPOLIS.

It looketh ill for thee to say such things
Of one who brought so much doth civilize.
Who taught us how to cure ourselves when ill ?

AETES.

Who but my mate ?   Being all-endowed, she brought
With her the leech's skill.   Bound'ries of land—
The cause of your complaint—were first set up
By her advice ; she saw ye planting here
And there and everywhere, the flocks and herds
Roaming at will and trampling all the land,
And said *enclosures would be good.*   Had she

Not come, ye never would have thought to claim
Each man his land, to have disputes about.

SOPOLIS.

Thou 'dst better take thy mate up to the mount
And leave her there, the other side the hedge.
We want no woman round, nor yet to hear
What she doth *say*, nor what she *knows*.   Full soon
Thou 'lt bring her here to *sit* with us, and *speak !*
                    [*Laughs derisively.*

MICCUS.

A woman's honey tongue would wile a god.

AETES.

I ofttimes think, could she be here, that ye
Would speak like men, not bellow forth like bulls.
To her own land I 'll not give up her right.
                    [*To* SOPOLIS.
But that I 'm counsellor here, the choice of all,
I 'd beat thee black and blue.   [*To the rest.*] Your
     quarrels now
Decide yourselves.   I will not come again
Till she can come with me, speak for herself.

POLITES.

I trust thou wilt not leave us.   Let us talk
The matter over, settle it in peace.

AETES.

Among yourselves ye may.   I 'll bide the result. ·
　　　[*Exit.*   DION *takes* AETES' *seat.*

SOPOLIS.

If *she* doth come, then will not *I* again.

MICCUS.

I 'll stay away !

DOLOPS.
　　　　　And if we let her come,
Who 'll keep the hut ?

CLEON.
　　　　　When she doth *ask* to come
'T is time enough to say we 'll have her here.

SOPOLIS.

We 'll have no woman here.

POLITES.
　　　　　　　　　　It seemeth me
It is not right to treat her thus.   I think
Her influence doth make us what we are.
Before she came we lived in caves, like bears,
Nor built we huts till after she appeared.
We sowed broadcast the barley, lentils, wheat ;
It sprang up where it listed.   When 't was ripe
We sorted it, and weeks it took to lay

The barley here, the millet there, the wheat,
All separate upon the threshing place.

PELIAS.

She taught us how to make the barley cake,
Stirred up with olive oil and milk ; preserve
The figs, dipped first in honey, and laid by
For Winter's use (to flavor porridge with) ;
To curdle, bind the milk with fig-tree juice.
She taught us fish to salt, and how to sew
Our garments firmly with the ox-hide thews.

POLITES.

'T would do no harm, methinks, to let her come ;
If she doth have a right to land, she ought
To state her claim.   We tell our grievances,—
They 're heard and fairly judged.   Why should not
     she ?
We owe her this, if not for justice's sake,—
For that she helps us to improve our lot.

DION, *to* PELIAS.

Wouldst thou not have thy way against her will ?
Wouldst thou not rule ?   Should she not thee obey ?

PELIAS.

I should say not.   Her way might be as good,
Her will tend to the right, as well as mine ;
Then why should she obey ?

POLITES.

We each should learn
Of each ; respect each other's ways, nor e'er
Coerce ; I ever try to learn of thee, [*to* PELIAS]
I like to learn.　And why not learn of her ?
I 'd gladly learn of her, had I a mate !
Ah, me ! where is the mate of whom I speak !
Would that she lived,—for me.

DION.

Thou wouldst be led,
Coerced !

POLITES.

Mayhap, and yet I 'm not so sure !
We should confer and counsel each with each.
When I thought she was right, I should agree.
'T would be the same with her.　I 'd like to have
Pandora here.　I like Aetes' ways,
And know he could not be the man he is,—
Our judge, our counsellor,—without her help,
Without the discipline their children bring
Into their lives.

DION.

We 've heard enough of this !
Now let us hear what Bias hath to say.
He 's big with speech.

BIAS.

She is not strong enough ;
Nor can she wrestle, pitch the quoit, nor run
To reach the goal.   She cannot plough, fell trees,
The slow-back oxen drive, or chase the boar,
The wild bull conquer, catch the ebon mares
That up the craggy side of Ossa fly
With snorting lip and streaming tail and mane.

DION.

She cannot fight, nor yet protect herself.
She surely should not speak !

BIAS.

She doth not eat
So much as one of us, nor yet the same.
She will not eat raw flesh ; she cooks her meat
With fire.   How can she be as strong as we ?

DION.

She 's small, her frame, her head, her voice is less,
Far less than ours : therefore she must not speak.

STILPO (*the old man*).

Look at the ills she brought !   We ne'er knew toil
Before she came.   The labor of one day
Would yield enough of food to last a year.
No ague hot, nor errors of the flesh
Did make our old bones ache, eh—heugh !

These ills
Pandora brought—and cannot cure—do make
My life most hard to bear.   If she comes here,
She 'll bring on us a thousand more as bad.

CLEON.

Jove meant not she should speak.   'Tis 'gainst his
    will.
No woman's voice was heard when gods and men
Assembled on the day he sent her forth.
Nor did he give consent that she should come
To gatherings of men ; she must not come !

POLITES.

If she the weaker is, more reason then
That we should justice do.   The strong should heed
The suppliant's cry, the weak one's pleading voice.

ASBOLUS.

Hold thou !   Let this prevail !   Thy arguments
Are good enough, but mine o'ertops them all.
She is a woman !   That is cause enough,
Good reason why she should not speak, nor join
Our councils.   Jove did make her for a curse,
A snare inextricable, source of hurt,
A seeming good, but a pernicious ill.
He made her vain, and with a treacherous mind.

POLITES.

Go to ! Thou 'st said enough ! I 'll hear no more !
[*Exit.*

ASBOLUS.

My sack is not yet empty, nor my bin—
A baneful care ; she fills the earth with woe ;
Keeps blessed Hope still fugitive and lost ;
Makes misery's crushing hand seize all our lives
And woes innumerable roam the world.

PELIAS.

I, too, have heard enough ! Thou boor ! thou cur !
Thou coward, ever brave when there 's no need !
Thou railer 'gainst the weak ! thou blatant foe
Of woman ! Be assured the time will come
When thou must answer all thou 'st said 'gainst her.
[*Exit.*

ASBOLUS.

Her being woman—dost not see—is cause
Sufficient, that she should not come, nor plead
Her claim, her right to her inheritance
In gatherings of men ? She shall not come !

CLEON.

Aetes strong,—what if he doth insist ?
His strength doth vanquish all. His voice per-
suades
Men's minds against their will. The straight he
bends,

The weak he props, the crooked he doth raise,
Supports the toppling, leads us all at will.
And then, urbane Polites, Pelias just,
Are on his side.   I fear they will prevail.

MICCUS, *in terror.*

If she comes here, the world will all go wrong.
The goats will stray ; the ewes set on by dogs ;
The cows will all be out of time ; the figs
Be stole ; more women come ; bound'ries let loose ;
Altars be raised to Jove in every place ;
Olympus turned to grass and all burned up !

STILPO.

When that time comes, O let us thankful be
Not many of us will be there to see !

SCENE III.—*An inner room in the hut.* PANDORA
alone, wearily planning a coat of skins.

Enter AETES, *angrily.*

AETES.

What dost thou think ?   Sopolis claimed thy land !
Contending 'gainst my right to plant the trees
So near the heavenly mount.   *My mate,* I said,
*Deems all the land that borders on that side
Belongs to her,—'t is her inheritance.*
Then he set up a shout, and others drowned

My voice.   With speeches mean they taunted thee
(All but Polites kind and Pelias just)
That thou art woman ; and this roused my ire.
I raged and left them, saying angrily :
I 'll ne'er come back till ye do send for her
To speak her right.   I 'll not go there again !

PANDORA.

For that men do not let me sit with them
And have a voice about mine own affairs,
It is no cause thou shouldst thy duty shirk.
I trust thou wilt return.

AETES.

What right had he
To claim thy land ? 'T is that thou 'rt *woman*, dear.
He would not dare to claim a rood from me !

PANDORA.

He had no *right*.   'T is *might* that rules with him.

AETES.

Why shouldst thou not go there with me ?   Thou
    goest
All otherwhere ?

PANDORA.

Thou know'st I little care
What bounds my scope, what my possessions are

This side the mount.   'T is more to me what lies
Beyond.   And yet, for my dear children's sake,
I much desire to keep, to have them keep,
The ground that touches all my heavenly home—
My true inheritance, and theirs through me.

AETES.

And thou shalt keep it !   They shall never touch
A single spot.   It shall descend to all
Thy race, and they shall ever have the right
To plant the tree that yields the bread of life.

PANDORA.

If I should go, it would not be to claim
My land, so much as tell them what I see
Upon the farther side ; that men may live
As tho' they too were heirs, and might sometime
Possess the mount.   Would I might show the way !
Would I could tell them that those heavenly heights
Hold in their teeming sides a boon more rare
Than olive-trees, than lentils, fields of corn !
Would I were strong, like thee, and that my sex
No hindrance were to me !

AETES.

                    I think it not !
If I in youth, advantage o'er thee had,
Now, older grown, thou more than equal art.
Thy womanhood made thee to see the right,

While yet my manhood grovelled far below.
I had to fight for mastery o'er myself,
But thou didst conquer by thy nature pure.

PANDORA.

Give me no praise for that to earth I brought
Th' intuitive sense ; I but the medium am
By which the woman element came down
To earth. 'T is different far from man ; but yet
No better and no worse. 'T is not confined
To me, nor to Harmonia, for my son
Is feminine, my daughter like to thee.

AETES.

Sex hath no limitations thou need'st fear !
For in itself, believe me, it is naught.
The quality of mind is all. I note
That we, tho' man and woman, are alike.
We eat and drink, we sleep and wake ; our wants
Are all the same ; we must be clothed. And both
Alike must suffer if we sin. We ask
For justice ; we are parents ; all our lives
Are bound in one. Alone we should be naught.
To us, our children dear a likeness bear,
E'en as we are the blended likenesses
Of Him, the father,—mother, of mankind.
And so I think that thou shouldst say thy word
Concerning thine own land. But if thou think'st
'T is better not—for fear of broils and words

Much better left unsaid—why, I will go
Alone, and tell them what thou sayst.   And so
From very shame they may at last consent.
But if they do not, we will little care ;
The time will come when they will wish thee there.

ACT V.

ACT V.

ACT V.

CHARLICO.

Would I were happy, as my sister is.
Or as in that supremest hour when Hope
First spoke to me. What is this happiness?
This permeating force, intangible,
That filled the inmost fibre of my life,
That fed each tissue, satisfied my soul?
But now 't is gone, and hunger doth consume
My being's core, and saps its fount of life.

[*Scatters flowers on the casket. Enter* PANDORA.

PANDORA.

Arouse, my son! Look not within thyself
With introverted gaze. Look up! No more
Brood o'er thy thoughts, thy imaginary griefs.
Thou must not think that beauty dwells on earth
Alone for thee. The hind that turns the clod
And bends to his low task, sees beauty too.
For him, the crested thistle rears its fronds,

135

The gentian's fringes droop, the azalea blooms ;
He sees the star-flower rear its gilded rays,
The moonlit clethra wave its feathery leaves ;
To welcome his approach corydalis nods.
Thou hast no right to waste thy manhood thus.
The beautiful 't is well to seek and love,
But thou must also heed stern duty's voice :
It binds in closest bonds all earthly things.

CHARLICO.

I am not, cannot be, the useful kind.

PANDORA.

The useful kind is good, hath qualities
That thou should'st imitate, not criticise.
They do the needful work for those who dream
And let the world go by.   The dreamer's life
Is sweet ; 't is also weak, enervating.
He only tops fair Pindus' height, who climbs
Its rugged sides.

CHARLICO *sighs.*

   I 'm on the heights full oft,
And in the depths.   I 've known the greatest bliss,
Been sunk in sorrow deeper than the sea.

PANDORA.

My son ! who helps his kind, and works his best,
Is greater far than he who idly dreams.

[Aside.

Unhappy boy !   How can I teach to him
What I in vain have tried to teach myself ?

[A soft strain proceeds from the casket.

CHARLICO.

What sound doth fill the air !

PANDORA.

I hear no sound,
Save in the distant tree the wood-bird sings,
And o'er its sandy nest the swallow makes
Her soft melodious plaint.

CHARLICO.

[Aside.
Would I could tell !

PANDORA.

My son, what aileth thee ?   What lights thy face ?
It gleams and glows.   'T is like the ascending sun,
Through cloudy bars, high-piled.   Or yet, the fire
Prometheus brought that shines in chambers dim.

CHARLICO.

It means, O mother, I a mate shall have !
It means that thou, ere snows shall crown thine age,
Wilt gain what thou hast longed for all thy life !

It means, thy son no more shall dwell alone !
It means, O joy ! that o'er the impatient world
A blessing hid from man will be unfurled.

SCENE II.—*Outside the hut. Autumn foliage. The
ilex-tree stands as in Act I., Scene V.* PANDORA
*comes from the hut slowly and wearily, and sits on a
rustic seat beneath the tree.*

PANDORA *aside.*

How like a flame burns that bright golden tree !
When first I came to earth 't was early spring ;
The fig-tree's leaf was like the dove's small foot,
And rosy-pointed buds, upon the oak
Had burst.   But now, in autumn colors dressed,
It stands.   'T is like a woman crowned with love,
Who waits the annunciation of a life
That will be born of her—her perfect flower.
And so I stand, but all my yellowing leaves,
In this still autumn eve, do drop and drop
On mother earth, who gladly welcomes them.
I can but trust that in me lies the germ
Of everlasting being, to bud and grow
In newer, rounder life ; but yet myself,—
As is the tree that lives and dies each year,
But after its own kind, and still the same.
I feel my end is near.   All night in dreams
I held the child, and up Olympus' side
I toiled and groped along.   When at the top

Appeared my very self, but young and fair,
Just as when down the way to earth I came,
Led by swift Mercury, and crowned with flowers.
(How my contractile feet the soft mead spurned !)
To this fair shape I gave the little child ;
It vanished, leaving me a heavy clod.
Jove ! Let me not return to thee, until
Through me, my race receives a crowning good.

> [*She kneels under the ilex-tree.*

PANDORA'S PRAYER.

Great Jove ! 't is I, Pandora, mother of my kind.
I heed thy message clear, sent me by Hypnos pale.
I ask thee not that this my life may be prolonged,
That I may live again among the immortal gods.
But this I ask, that I may be allowed by thee
To do one single thing to make my kind more
    good,
More happy for that I have lived. Thou madest me
The source, the messenger of ills to man. But I
Have learned thy true intent, interpreted thy
    thought—
That, 'neath each seeming ill, a hidden blessing
    lies.
And what I could do, that I did, to obey thy will.
This legacy would I bequeath, this one pure gift
To all my race,—I fain would bid sweet Hope come
    forth.

Let me not die while still the only good lies hid
Within the casket's verge.   O, let me bid it forth !
If thou dost think me worthy of the boon, O hear
My supplication, Father, hearken to my cry !

SCENE III.—*Inside the hut.   The loom is set
against the wall.   The cradle is gone.   The casket
is drawn to the front, and is covered with autumn
flowers.* PANDORA *sits with her distaff, in a listless
attitude.   Enter* AETES.

AETES.

Why, thou dost weep !   What ails my dearest mate ?
Thou look'st as when the first-born child laid
        there—
(Not all my cries could wake its slumbers deep).

PANDORA.

Aetes, I was not to blame ?   I sinned
Unknowingly.

AETES.

                I blamed thee not ; 't was I !
I was to blame !

PANDORA.

                No, I ! I loved it not.
'T was this that killed the child.   It drank my tears ;
'T was lulled to sleep with my repining song.
It died for lack of mother-love : no child,
No youngling, e'er can thrive that yearns for this.

AETES.

Thou did'st not know, how could'st thou know,
    thy grief
Would wither, sap the source of all its life?

PANDORA.

How have I mourned! Ah, me! how strange it is!
Life's mystery is this : What parents do
Is mirrored in their children ; changeless laws
Proclaim, that neither intercession, prayer,
Nor yet repentance, can atone for deeds
By parents done,—transgressions of the flesh.
'T is sins like these will cheat mankind of half
His heritage ; take from his nerves the steel,
His bones the marrow, rob his brain of strength.

AETES.

Grieve not so much. Thou 'dst scarce begun to
    learn
Oh, how much living doth it take, before
A soul can from the flesh arise new-born,
Unhindered by its clay! Thou found'st me on
The lowest plane of life ; me hast thou raised,
Uplifted unto heights ne'er known to man.

PANDORA.

And thou hast lifted me. We could not rise
Alone ; thy wings of love have me upborne.
And though I oft regret the ills I brought—

AETES.

The ills are naught.   The good that thou hast
    brought
Outweighs them all a thousand times.   Mayhap
'T was Jove's intent.   Before thou cam'st, a clod,
An undeveloped soul was I ; these ills
Have made me man, of Jove's high attributes
Inheritor.   This marvel thou hast wrought.

PANDORA.

More hast thou wrought for me.   A puling maid,
Unsatisfied was I, complaining oft
Of my sad lot.   Thou hast developed me
And made to bloom the soul that in the bud
Infolded lay, nor knew if it were weed
Or flower.   Thou art my strength, my comforter,
Now, in mine age, when I am faded, wan.

AETES.

Thou art my flower whose blossoms span the year.

PANDORA.

No more I welcome thee with gayest steps,
But feeble, tottering, scarce thy neck can reach.
No more the web grows 'neath my skilful hands ;
My loom is silent, and my shuttle stays
Where last I left it, tangled in the web.
No more the morning breaks in songs, the light
Is gone from Ossa's mount and Pindus' top.

AETES.

Mourn not, my mate, for thou hast done enough.
Thou never canst be old.   A light within
Thine eyes doth rise to greet me, younger far
Than day's first beam.   Thou canst not change to
   me.
For in mine eyes thou 'rt ever young and fair,
And home thou mak'st the brightest place on earth.

PANDORA.

How blest the wedded home where friendship
   reigns !
Its walls coherent are with light and warmth ;
Within its depths dwell comfort, patience, love.
There hides no sin, nor aught contaminate.
Freedom of speech is welcomed there, and each
Is just to each.   There order, neatness rules,
As meets the needs of all.   No single one
Lays down the law that will coerce the rest.
'T is not too finely kept for daily use.
The noble souls that in it dwell, go forth
To their appointed task ; and they return,
With joyful hearts, as do the gods, to seek
Their sleeping-place, their many-chambered rest.
Thither, in sacred silence of the night,
The spirit of its dead may glad return,
And o'er the sleeping one, with loving kiss
May bend, sure that the memory of no deed
Unworthy, no unfaithful thought, can come

Between their souls to mar the perfect bliss
Of such serene communion. [*She bows her head.*]
This, dear love !
This is the wedded home, thine own, and mine.

AETES, *in alarm.*

What dost thou mean ? Return ? Thou 'lt not
leave me ?

PANDORA, *after a moment.*

I would not willingly, but I am called.

AETES.

Who called thee ? Thou 'lt not go ; thou canst·not
go ?

PANDORA.

But Jove hath called me through the gate of dreams.

AETES.

Thou wouldst not leave me here,—to live alone ?

PANDORA.

Unless Jove wills.   This only do I know :
A vision came before my sleeping eyes.
I stood upon a height, just as I stood
Ere yet my pulsing veins were filled with life,
And there to me a shape appeared, that said :
Thou wilt go back to thy remembered home.

This life 's a hut made for thy dwelling-place
A few short years, and through its open door
Are glimpses seen of yet another home ;
Or, 't is a hedge so green that bounds thy scope
Along whose bosky side ye walk, and like
Th' impounded deer, an outlet seek. This life
Is closely welded to the life beyond.
Be sure of this : there is no break, no break !

AETES.

How shall I know thee there ; if on the earth
I stay, till old and worn, and blind mayhap
As I may be ?

PANDORA.

Wouldst thou not know my voice,
My touch, my hand ?

AETES.

Yes, I should know thy voice,
Tho' blended with the myriad angels' song ;
Thy touch would thrill me, tho' a hundred years
Eternal blindness darkened all my world ;
My hand thine own would find, would recognize,
E'en though 't were stretched with thousand wel-
    coming ones.

PANDORA.

So should I thine ! We need not fear to part !

AETES.

Then am I reconciled. This world is good—
So good, I fain would stay here, love, with thee—
But if the other is its counterpart,
It is enough. Forget me not! Grow not
Away from me!

PANDORA.

Whatever happeneth, dear,
I e'er shall love thee, ever long for thee.
If I could know that I might bid sweet Hope
Come forth to dwell with those I leave on earth,
Then could I almost willing go. Ah me!
Am I *subdued, uplifted, disciplined,*
Refined, as Epimetheus said? I doubt.

AETES.

As much as woman can be, sure art thou.
But I 'm not good enough to walk with thee.

PANDORA.

Thou art. Let us be just. Whate'er we lack,
We both are sure of this : that we *do know*
The meaning of our lives.

AETES.

Thy love taught me.
How can we part ! How can I let thee go !

PANDORA.

My steadfast mate ! Now is the time full near
When all will be fulfilled. He knoweth best
Who rules.

> [*Enter* CHARLICO, OLEN, *and* HARMONIA. *Soft
> music sounds from the casket;* CHARLICO
> *springs toward it; it falls slowly apart and
> Hope, ever young and fair, arises.* CHARLICO
> *takes her right hand,* HARMONIA *her left, and
> they lead her to* PANDORA. *PANDORA rises.*

Joy ! Joy ! My children bring me Hope !

CHARLICO.

Dear mother, grieve no more, for here is Hope.
And mourn no more the ills thou brought'st to earth.
Hope hast thou also brought, the longed-for good.
'T is she completes the rounded score of life.
I am content. She fills my soul. What more
Can man desire, for Hope is in the world ?
Her heavenly smile will drive away all ills,
Beneath all pain and sorrow she will bide,
Will lead the spirit to its heavenly home.

PANDORA.

I thank and bless thee, O almighty Jove,
Thou hast created me ! For now I see
That thou didst mean me for the messenger

Of good to man.   And now I know, for that
I woman am, doth not confine my scope.
Sex cannot limit the immortal mind.
We are ourselves, with individual souls,
Still struggling onward toward the infinite.

> [*To* AETES.

Would we might go together !

AETES.

> Would we might !

> [*The hut expands.   At the back stands Olympus.
> The gate of clouds is seen a little way up its
> side, guarded by the Hours.   Shadowy figures
> pass and repass behind it ; one, a beautiful
> maiden, stands near the gate, and holds out
> both hands.   A path leads upward from the
> hut.   A soft prelude is sounded,—" Come
> away "—as in* ACT II., SCENE IV.

Song of the Child-Spirit.

Come away, mother dear, to the beautiful land,
  Come and rest in its chambers of peace ;
'T is thy first-born that calls thee, her beckoning
    hand
  Entreats thy worn spirit's release.

> Come away.

Come away ; God is good. 'Neath his sheltering
    care,
  Lives thy little one, lost long ago ;
Behold her a maiden immortal and fair,
  Only happiness, joy, doth she know.
                         Come away.

Come away ; through the cloud-gate the bright
    pathway lies,
  Far away from all sorrow and pain.
Come, follow thy child to her home in the skies,
  Reunited forever again.
                         Come away.

       PANDORA, *to her children.*

Grieve not for me ; this life is lived.   I leave
With thee the greatest good.   This have I gained
Through pain and sorrowing still unknown to thee.
                      [*To* AETES.
My love !   Dear mate of my undying life,
Not willingly I leave thee here alone.
But soon thou 'lt follow me, farewell ! farewell !

    [HOPE *advances and points to the gate.* PANDORA
      toils painfully up the path. AETES *springs*
      after her and falls. PANDORA *turns, takes*
      his hand, raises him, and they walk on together,
      and enter the gate of clouds, which closes behind
      them.

HOPE, *still pointing.*

Ever the heart of the mother will yearn
Upward, to follow the lead of the child.

[*She turns to* CHARLICO, *and unclasps her cestus
in token that she gives herself to him.* HAR-
MONIA *falls on the breast of* OLEN. *Olympus
is shut in and they are left in the hut.*

Song of the Immortals.

SEMICHORUS.

Thou hast conquered !   Rise triumphant
Upward toward thy being's sun,
All the world is changed, uplifted,
For the life that thou hast won.

CHORUS.

Rise, O rise, ye souls immortal !
Break, O break, imprisoning clay !
Pass, ye heavenly guests, pass onward ;
Hope, exultant, points the way.

SEMICHORUS.

Suffering is the great redeemer,
Joy and pain together bide ;
'T was to save from sin and sorrow,
The little first-born child hath died.

CHORUS.

Rise, O rise, ye souls immortal !
  Break, O break, imprisoning clay !
Pass, ye heavenly guests, pass onward,
  Hope, exultant, points the way.